全民英語能力分級檢定測驗

中級英語檢定複試測驗①

寫作能力測驗

本測驗共有兩部份。第一部份爲中譯英，第二部份爲英文作文。測驗時間爲 **40分鐘**。

一、中譯英（40%）

說明：請將下列的一段中文翻譯成通順、達意且前後連貫的英文。

　　小時候，我常常在星期日的早晨陪媽媽上菜市場。在市場你可以看到各種商品，你也可以聽到人們討價還價，以及小販大聲招攬顧客的聲音。市場裡總是生氣勃勃的。過了一兩個小時後，媽媽就會買一些零嘴給我吃。老實說，我眞的很喜歡上市場。在市場裡，總是有新的事物可以觀看和學習。

二、英文作文（60%）

說明：請依下面所提供的文字提示寫一篇英文作文，長度約120字（8至12個句子）。作文可以是一個完整的段落，也可以分段。（評分重點包括內容、組織、文法、用字遣詞、標點符號、大小寫。）

提示：感冒的經驗人人都有，如何從感冒中恢復（How to Get Over a Cold）是很重要的。請寫一篇文章說明：
　　當你感冒時，你會怎麼做，讓自己的感冒快快好起來呢？

中級英檢寫作練習

口説能力測驗

請在 15 秒內完成並唸出下列自我介紹的句子：

My seat number is （複試座位號碼後 5 碼）, and my registration number is （初試准考證號碼後 5 碼）.

第一段份：朗讀短文

請先利用一分鐘的時間閱讀下面的短文，然後在二分鐘內以正常的速度，清楚正確的讀出下面的短文，閱讀時請不要發出聲音。

From early childhood, most of us have been taught that "anything worth doing is worth doing well." If we were asked today whether we still agree with the statement, many of us would say we do. It is only natural for a person to prefer a job that has been done well to one that has not been done so well. It is also easy to see why a person may not like to redo something that has already been done, particularly if the combined time involved is greater than the time that would have been required to do it right in the first place.

*　　　　　　*　　　　　　*

In downtown Washington, almost midway between the Capitol and the White House stand two historic buildings—Ford's Theatre and the house where Lincoln died. In Ford's Theatre, on the evening of April 14, 1865, Lincoln was shot by John Wilkes Booth. Early the next morning the President died in the Peterson House, directly across the street from the theatre. In his death, as in his life, Abraham Lincoln entered deeply into the folklore and history of our country. He has become a symbol to us and to the world of the heights to which a common man can reach.

Ford's Theatre and the Peterson House carry the visitor back to the days of the Civil War and to one of our nation's saddest nights.

第二部份：回答問題

共十題。題目已事先錄音，每題經由耳機播出二次，不印在試卷上。第一至五題，每題回答時間 15 秒；第六至十題，每題回答時間 30 秒。每題播出後，請立即回答。回答時，不一定要用完整的句子，但請在作答時間內儘量的表達。

第三部份：看圖敘述

下面有一張圖片及四個相關的問題，請在一分半鐘內完成作答。作答時，請直接回答，不需將題號及題目唸出。

首先請利用 30 秒的時間看圖及問題。

1. 這可能是什麼地方？
2. 這裡的環境如何？
3. 圖裡的人在做什麼？
4. 請敘述圖片中人物正在進行的活動以及他們的感受。

請將下列自我介紹的句子再唸一遍：

My seat number is（<u>複試座位號碼後 5 碼</u>），and my registration number is（<u>初試准考證號碼後 5 碼</u>）.

口說能力測驗解答

第一部份：朗讀短文

請先利用一分鐘的時間閱讀下面二篇短文，閱讀時請不要發出聲音，然後在二分鐘之內以正常的速度，清楚正確的讀出下面的短文。

From early childhood, most of us have been taught that "anything worth doing is worth doing well." If we were asked today whether we still agree with the statement, many of us would say we do. It is only natural for a person to prefer a job that has been done well to one that has not been done so well. It is also easy to see why a person may not like to redo something that has already been done, particularly if the combined time involved is greater than the time that would have been required to do it right in the first place.

【註】 ***be worth V-ing*** 值得～　　statement〔'stetmənt〕*n.* 敘述
prefer A ***to*** B 喜歡 A 甚於 B　　redo〔ri'du〕*v.* 重做
combine〔kəm'baɪn〕*v.* 結合　　involve〔ɪn'vɑlv〕*v.* 需要
require〔rɪ'kwaɪr〕*v.* 需要　　right〔raɪt〕*adv.* 正確地
in the first place 當初；最初

In downtown Washington, almost midway between the Capitol and the White House stand two historic buildings— Ford's Theatre and the house where Lincoln died. In Ford's Theatre, on the evening of April 14, 1865, Lincoln was shot by John Wilkes Booth. Early the next morning the President died in the Peterson House, directly across the street from the theatre. In his death, as in his life, Abraham Lincoln entered deeply into the folklore and history of our country. He has become a symbol to us and to the world of the heights to which a common man can reach. Ford's Theatre and the Peterson House carry the visitor back to the days of the Civil War and to one of our nation's saddest nights.

【註】 downtown〔'daʊn'taʊn〕*adj.* 市中心的
midway〔'mɪd,we〕*adv.* 在中途
Capitol〔'kæpətl̩〕*n.* 國會大廈
the White House 白宮 (美國總統官邸)
stand〔stænd〕*v.* 聳立著
historic〔hɪs'tɔrɪk〕*adv.* 有歷史性的　　theatre〔'θiətɚ〕*n.* 戲院
shoot〔ʃut〕*v.* 射殺 (三態變化為：shoot-shot-shot)
John Wilkes Booth〔'dʒɑn 'wɪlks 'buθ〕*n.* 約翰・威爾克斯・布思
directly〔də'rɛktlɪ〕*adv.* 直接地；正好
across〔ə'krɔs〕*prep.* 在～對面
directly across the street from 在…的正對面
folklore〔'fok,lor〕*n.* 民間傳說　　symbol〔'sɪmbl̩〕*n.* 象徵
heights〔haɪts〕*n. pl.* 高處；頂峰
civil〔'sɪvl̩〕*adj.* 國內的；公民的
the Civil War (美國) 南北戰爭

第二部份：回答問題

Question 1 : *Did you exercise this morning? Why or why not?*

Answer : Yes, I did.

I exercise every morning.

Exercise is part of my daily routine.

Exercise gives me energy.

Exercise makes me feel great.

It's a healthy thing to do.

daily〔'delɪ〕*adj.* 日常的；每天的

routine〔ru'tin〕*n.* 例行公事　　energy〔'ɛnɚdʒɪ〕*n.* 活力

healthy〔'hɛlθɪ〕*adj.* 健康的

Question 2 : *How was the weather yesterday? Did you like it?*

Answer : Yesterday was beautiful.

Yesterday's weather was fantastic.

It was clear and sunny all day.

The weather was perfect.

The temperature was just right.

It was such a comfortable day.

fantastic〔fæn'tæstɪk〕*adj.* 極好的　　clear〔klɪr〕*adj.* 晴朗的

sunny〔'sʌnɪ〕*adj.* 陽光普照的　　perfect〔'pɝfɪkt〕*adj.* 完美的

temperature〔'tɛmprətʃɚ〕*n.* 溫度　　*just right* 剛剛好

Question 3 : *Will you buy any new clothes soon? Why or why not?*

Answer : Yes, I will.

I plan to go shopping.

I'm going to the mall this weekend.

I need some new shoes.

I need clothes for school.

I need to ask my parents for money.

go shopping 去購物　　mall〔mɔl〕*n.* 購物中心
ask sb. for sth. 向某人要求某物

Question 4 : *When would you normally take a bus and when would you take a taxi?*

Answer : I normally take a bus to school.

I usually take a bus with my friends.

I only take taxis in certain situations.

I take a taxi when I'm late.

I take a taxi if I'm in a hurry.

I take a taxi if the weather is bad.

normally〔'nɔrmḷɪ〕*adv.* 通常

certain〔'sɝtṇ〕*adj.* 某些　　situation〔,sɪtʃʊ'eʃən〕*n.* 情況

in a hurry 匆忙；趕時間

Question 5 : *How often do you stay up late? Why do you do it?*

Answer : I stay up late every night.

I like the evening hours.

I'm a real night owl.

It's the perfect time to study.

I really hit the books.

I burn the midnight oil.

stay up 熬夜　　hours〔aʊrz〕*n. pl.* 時間

owl〔aʊl〕*n.* 貓頭鷹　　*night owl* 夜貓子；晚睡的人

hit the books K書　　*burn the midnight oil* 熬夜；開夜車

Question 6 : *Do you think you will receive any presents*

for your next birthday? Why or why not?

Answer : I know I will.

My friends never forget.

My family never lets me down.

I always get some gifts.

Everyone is so generous.

Everyone likes to show they care.

let sb. down 使某人失望（ = *disappoint sb.* ）

generous〔'dʒɛnərəs〕*adj.* 慷慨的；大方的

care〔kɛr〕*v.* 在乎

Question 7 : *What can parents do to prevent their children from watching too much TV?*

Answer : Parents can do a lot.

Parents can set rules.

Parents can set time-watching limits.

They can impose discipline.

They can encourage healthier activities.

They can spend more time with their kids.

set〔sɛt〕*v.* 設定　　limit〔ˈlɪmɪt〕*n.* 限制
impose〔ɪmˈpoz〕*v.* 強加；施行
discipline〔ˈdɪsəplɪn〕*n.* 紀律；訓練
encourage〔ɪnˈkɝɪdʒ〕*v.* 鼓勵

Question 8 : *Is this test easier or more difficult than you expected? Please explain.*

Answer : This test is much easier.

It's a piece of cake.

It's not as tough as I thought.

Some parts were too easy.

Some areas were really simple.

Thank God I over-prepared.

a piece of cake 容易之事　　tough〔tʌf〕*adj.* 困難的
area〔ˈɛrɪə〕*n.* 地區；地方
over-prepare〔ˌovɚprɪˈpɛr〕*v.* 過度準備

Question 9 : *If you could study abroad in either England or America, which would you prefer and why?*

Answer : I'd prefer the U.S.A.

I have friends and relatives there.

I'd feel more comfortable in America.

I'd choose America.

American English is more colorful.

American English is more fun to learn.

prefer〔prɪˋfɝ〕*v.* 比較喜歡　　relative〔ˋrɛlətɪv〕*n.* 親戚
fun〔fʌn〕*adj.* 有趣的　　colorful〔ˋkʌləfəl〕*adj.* 多采多姿的

Question 10 : *Have you used a computer before? What are some advantages and disadvantages of using a computer?*

Answer : Yes, of course I have.

I use computers all the time.

I enjoy surfing the Web and e-mailing friends.

Computers are ideal for research.

Computers are great entertainment.

The only bad thing is they waste a lot of time.

advantage〔ədˋvæntɪdʒ〕*n.* 優點
disadvantage〔͵dɪsədˋvæntɪdʒ〕*n.* 缺點
surf the Web 上網；瀏覽網站（= *surf the Internet*）
ideal〔aɪˋdiəl〕*adj.* 理想的　　research〔ˋrisɝtʃ〕*n.* 研究
entertainment〔͵ɛntəˋtenmənt〕*n.* 娛樂

第三部份:看圖敘述

1. This is a picture of a computer classroom.

2. You can see a couple of computers on the desk.

3. The people in the picture are singing in two groups.

4 The people in the computer classroom are tired of using computers. They decided to have some fun. They hooked up some microphones and loaded a KTV program on the computer. Then they chose and sang songs. In this picture we can see they sang in two groups: three in one and two in the other. It didn't matter whether they were good singers or awful ones. They all had a good time that day.

【註】 *a couple of* 幾個;數個 (= *several*)
be tired of 厭倦   *have fun* 玩得愉快 (= *have a good time*)
hook up 安裝;接上   microphone 〔'maɪkrə,fon 〕 *n.* 麥克風
load 〔 lod 〕 *v.* 裝上   program 〔'progræm 〕 *n.* 程式;節目
matter 〔'mætə 〕 *v.* 重要   awful 〔'ɔful 〕 *adj.* 糟糕的

全民英語能力分級檢定測驗

中級英語檢定複試測驗②

寫作能力測驗

本測驗共有兩部份。第一部份為中譯英，第二部份為英文作文。測驗時間為 **40分鐘**。

一、中譯英（40％）

說明：　請將下列的一段中文翻譯成通順、達意且前後連貫的英文。

　　　　英文諺語說：「天助自助者。」這句話說明了自助的重要性。換句話說，我們做事不可以依賴他人。如果一個人什麼事都依賴他人，他自己就不會努力工作，如果他不努力，又怎麼會成功呢？因此，我們必須用自己的力量來達成我們的目標。最後的勝利一定是屬於我們的。

二、英文作文（60％）

說明：　請依下面所提供的文字提示寫一篇英文作文，長度約120字（8至12個句子）。作文可以是一個完整的段落，也可以分段。（評分重點包括內容、組織、文法、用字遣詞、標點符號、大小寫。）

提示：　動物園是最受小朋友歡迎的地方之一，去動物園郊遊常常是家庭或是學校會舉辦的活動。請寫一篇文章描述你某次到動物園的經驗（A Visit to the Zoo）：你看到什麼、做什麼，有何感想。

中級英檢寫作練習

口説能力測驗

請在 15 秒內完成並唸出下列自我介紹的句子：

My seat number is （複試座位號碼後 5 碼）, and my registration number is （初試准考證號碼後 5 碼）.

第一段份：朗讀短文

請先利用一分鐘的時間閱讀下面的短文，然後在二分鐘內以正常的速度，清楚正確的讀出下面的短文，閱讀時請不要發出聲音。

I enjoy my job very much. I have a great chance to meet and talk to all kinds of people every day. Many people ask me questions, and I give them the necessary information. I try to be very helpful. I always call out floors very clearly, and I am constantly on the move. Most men take off their hats in my car, and sometimes I have to tell passengers to put out their cigarettes. Some people smile at me, but others just ignore me. In fact, my life can be described as consisting of a series of "ups" and "downs."

*　　　　　　　*　　　　　　　*

Most of us understand the results of not controlling our reactions to stress. Forty-three percent of all adults suffer terrible health effects from stress. Most physician office visits are for stress-related illnesses and complaints. Stress is linked to the six leading causes of death—heart disease, cancer, lung disease, accidents, liver disease, and suicide. Currently, health care costs account for about twelve percent of the gross domestic product.

第二部份：回答問題

共十題。題目已事先錄音，每題經由耳機播出二次，不印在試卷上。第一至五題，每題回答時間 15 秒；第六至十題，每題回答時間 30 秒。每題播出後，請立即回答。回答時，不一定要用完整的句子，但請在作答時間內儘量的表達。

第三部份：看圖敘述

下面有一張圖片及四個相關的問題，請在一分半鐘內完成作答。作答時，請直接回答，不需將題號及題目唸出。

首先請利用 30 秒的時間看圖及問題。

1. 這可能是什麼地方？
2. 這裡的環境如何？有什麼事物嗎？
3. 圖裡的人在做什麼？
4. 請敘述圖片中人物的活動以及景物。

請將下列自我介紹的句子再唸一遍：

My seat number is （複試座位號碼後 5 碼）, and my registration number is （初試准考證號碼後 5 碼）.

口說能力測驗解答

第一部份：朗讀短文

請先利用一分鐘的時間閱讀下面二篇短文，閱讀時請不要發出聲音，然後在二分鐘之內以正常的速度，清楚正確的讀出下面的短文。

I enjoy my job very much. I have a great chance to meet and talk to all kinds of people every day. Many people ask me questions, and I give them the necessary information. I try to be very helpful. I always call out floors very clearly, and I am constantly on the move. Most men take off their hats in my car, and sometimes I have to tell passengers to put out their cigarettes. Some people smile at me, but others just ignore me. In fact, my life can be described as consisting of a series of "ups" and "downs."

【註】 *call out* 叫喊；大聲說出　　floor〔flor〕*n.* 樓層
constantly〔'kɑnstəntlɪ〕*adv.* 不斷地　　*on the move* 移動中
take off 脫掉　　car〔kɑr〕*n.*（電梯的）機廂
passenger〔'pæsṇdʒɚ〕*n.* 乘客　　*put out* 熄滅
ignore〔ɪg'nor〕*v.* 忽視　　*in fact* 事實上
describe〔dɪ'skraɪb〕*v.* 描述；形容
consist of 由…組成
a series of 一連串的

　　Most of us understand the results of not controlling our reactions to stress.　Forty-three percent of all adults suffer terrible health effects from stress.　Most physician office visits are for stress-related illnesses and complaints.　Stress is linked to the six leading causes of death—heart disease, cancer, lung disease, accidents, liver disease, and suicide. Currently, health care costs account for about twelve percent of the gross domestic product.

【註】　reaction〔rɪˈækʃən〕n. 反應 < to >
　　　　stress〔strɛs〕n. 壓力（= pressure）
　　　　suffer〔ˈsʌfɚ〕v. 遭受
　　　　terrible〔ˈtɛrəbḷ〕adj. 可怕的；嚴重的
　　　　effect〔ɪˈfɛkt〕n. 影響　　physician〔fəˈzɪʃən〕n. 醫生
　　　　office〔ˈɔfɪs〕n. 診所　　visit〔ˈvɪzɪt〕n. 就診
　　　　related〔rɪˈletɪd〕adj. 有關的　　complaint〔kəmˈplent〕n. 疾病
　　　　link〔lɪŋk〕v. 連結　　**be linked to**　與～有關
　　　　leading〔ˈlidɪŋ〕adj. 主要的　　**cause of death**　死因
　　　　cancer〔ˈkænsɚ〕n. 癌症　　lung〔lʌŋ〕n. 肺
　　　　liver〔ˈlɪvɚ〕n. 肝臟　　suicide〔ˈsuəˌsaɪd〕n. 自殺
　　　　currently〔ˈkɝəntlɪ〕adv. 目前　　**health care**　醫療
　　　　account for　佔～（比例、數量等）
　　　　gross〔gros〕adj. 總共的
　　　　domestic〔dəˈmɛstɪk〕adj. 國內的
　　　　gross domestic product　國內生產毛額（= GDP）

第二部份：回答問題

Question 1 ： *How often does your family go out to eat?*

Answer ： We seldom eat out!

We all have different schedules.

It is hard for us to find time to eat out together.

Most of the time we eat at home.

Sometimes we order home delivery.

We eat out only on special occasions.

eat out 外出用餐　　schedule〔'skɛdʒul〕*n.* 時間表
order〔'ɔrdɚ〕*v.* 點菜；訂購　　delivery〔dɪ'lɪvərɪ〕*n.* 遞送
occasion〔ə'keʒən〕*n.* 場合；時候；特別的大事

Question 2 ： *Did you watch TV last night? Why or why not?*

Answer ： Of course, I watched TV.

I always watch news broadcasts.

I enjoy staying abreast of domestic and
    international news.

Television relaxes me.

It puts me at ease.

It also keeps me up to date.

broadcast〔'brɔd,kæst〕*n.* 廣播
abreast〔ə'brɛst〕*adv.* 並列地
stay abreast of 不落後；與…並駕齊驅
domestic〔də'mɛstɪk〕*adj.* 國內的　　relax〔rɪ'læks〕*v.* 使放鬆
put〔pʊt〕*v.* 使　　*at ease* 輕鬆地；悠閒地
up to date 不落後；切合目前的情況

Question 3： *Did you help your parents around the house last week? Why or why not?*

Answer： Yes, I helped my parents.

I always do my weekly chores.

I always help with the housecleaning.

My parents are both very busy.

We kids share the housework with them.

We try to lighten their load.

help around the house 幫忙家務

weekly〔'wiklɪ〕*adj.* 每週的   chores〔tʃɔrz〕*n. pl.* 雜事

housecleaning〔'haʊs,klinɪŋ〕*n.* 家庭清掃工作

share〔ʃɛr〕*v.* 分擔   housework〔'haʊs,wɜk〕*n.* 家事

lighten〔'laɪtn̩〕*v.* 減輕   load〔lod〕*n.* 負擔

Question 4： *How was the last movie you saw? Did you like it?*

Answer： It was an excellent production.

It was action-packed every minute.

The plot was well-developed.

It was thrilling from beginning to end.

I enjoyed the movie very much.

The movie was worth every penny!

production〔prə'dʌkʃən〕*n.* 製作

action-packed〔'ækʃən,pækt〕*adj.*（電影）內容豐富有趣的

plot〔plɑt〕*n.* 劇情

well-developed〔'wɛldɪ'vɛləpt〕*adj.* 制定得很完善的

thrilling〔'θrɪlɪŋ〕*adj.* 刺激的

from beginning to end 從頭到尾

penny〔'pɛnɪ〕*n.* 一分錢（= *cent*）

Question 5 : *What do you plan to do this summer? Please explain*.

Answer : My parents are planning a tour.

We might travel abroad.

We might spend two weeks overseas.

Besides, I plan to get a part-time job.

I want to earn some pocket money.

I will also study English at a cram school.

abroad〔ə'brɔd〕*adv.* 到國外

overseas〔'ovɚ'siz〕*adv.* 在國外

part-time〔'pɑrt,taɪm〕*adj.* 兼差的

pocket money 零用錢　　*cram school* 補習班

Question 6 : *How often do you go out with friends or classmates?*

Answer : We go out together very often.

We go out on a regular basis.

We enjoy snacking, chatting and window-shopping.

Sometimes we discuss our lessons.

Other times we just fool around doing nothing.

I like to hang out with my friends.

regular〔'rɛgjəlɚ〕*adj.* 定期的

on a regular basis 定期地（= *regularly*）

snack〔snæk〕*v.* 吃東西　　chat〔tʃæt〕*v.* 聊天

window-shop〔'wɪndo,ʃɑp〕*v.* 逛街瀏覽櫥窗

other times 有時　　*fool around* 閒混；虛度光陰

hang out 閒混；在一起

Question 7 : *Have you ever talked to a foreigner? How did you feel?*

Answer : Yes, I have.

I've chatted with foreigners a couple of times.

I think it's fun and exciting.

I was very nervous at first.

I was afraid to make mistakes.

Soon after, my worries disappeared.

a couple of 幾個（= *several*）　　nervous〔'nɜvəs〕*adj.* 緊張的
at first 起初　　*soon after* 不久之後　　worry〔'wɜɪ〕*n.* 擔心
disappear〔,dɪsə'pɪr〕*v.* 消失

Question 8 : *If you could have one wish, what would it be for and why?*

Answer : I'd wish for world peace.

I'd wish there were no more wars.

I'd like to terminate all violence and terrorism.

I'd like everyone to live in harmony.

I'd demand brotherhood for all.

Everybody should be treated equally and fairly.

wish for + N. 希望得到～　　peace〔pis〕*n.* 和平
terminate〔'tɜmə,net〕*v.* 終結　　violence〔'vaɪələns〕*n.* 暴力
terrorism〔'tɛrə,rɪzəm〕*n.* 恐怖主義；恐怖行為
harmony〔'harmənɪ〕*n.* 和諧　　demand〔dɪ'mænd〕*v.* 要求
brotherhood〔'brʌðə,hud〕*n.* 手足情誼　　treat〔trit〕*v.* 對待
equally〔'ikwəlɪ〕*adv.* 平等地　　fairly〔'fɛrlɪ〕*adv.* 公平地

Question 9 : *Do you think of yourself as a shy or outgoing person? Please explain.*

Answer : I'm a combination of both.

I have a complex personality.

I'm a tough person to figure out.

Sometimes I'm timid and bashful.

Sometimes I'm assertive and forceful.

It all depends on the environment and whom I'm with.

shy〔ʃaɪ〕*adj.* 害羞的　　outgoing〔ˌaʊt'goɪŋ〕*adj.* 外向的

combination〔ˌkɑmbə'neʃən〕*n.* 結合；綜合

complex〔kəm'plɛks〕*adj.* 複雜的（ = *complicated* ）

personality〔ˌpɝsn̩'ælətɪ〕*n.* 個性

tough〔tʌf〕*adj.* 困難的；難纏的　　*figure out* 了解

timid〔'tɪmɪd〕*adj.* 膽小的　　bashful〔'bæʃfəl〕*adj.* 害羞的

assertive〔ə'sɝtɪv〕*adj.* 有衝勁的

forceful〔'forsfəl〕*adj.* 強有力的；強勢的

depend on 視…而定；取決於

Question 10：*If you could live in a dormitory or with your parents, which would you prefer and why?*

Answer：I'd prefer living in a dorm.

I long for independence and freedom.

I'd like more interaction with my peers.

Dorm life is something of a challenge.

I could learn to cooperate and get along with others.

I could learn responsibility and respect for others.

dormitory〔'dɔrmə,torɪ〕*n.* 宿舍（ = *dorm* ）

long for 渴望　　independence〔ˌɪndɪ'pɛndəns〕*n.* 獨立

interaction〔ˌɪntɚ'ækʃən〕*n.* 互動 < *with* >

peer〔pɪr〕*n.* 同儕

something of a 可以說是；可以算得上；有點

challenge〔'tʃælɪndʒ〕*n.* 挑戰

cooperate〔ko'ɑpə,ret〕*v.* 合作

get along with sb. 與某人相處

第三部份：看圖敘述

1. This is a picture of a harbor.

2. It is a sunny day and there is a tall ship in the harbor. There are also some tall buildings in the distance.

3. In this picture many people are walking along the boardwalk.

4 Some people have come to see the tall ship anchored in the harbor. It is an unusual sight in the city. Other people are simply enjoying the fine weather. They stroll along the waterfront for exercise or to take a break in the middle of a busy day.

【註】harbor〔'hɑrbɚ〕 *n.* 港口　　sunny〔'sʌnɪ〕 *adj.* 晴朗的
in the distance 在遠方　　boardwalk〔'bord,wɔk〕 *n.* 海邊散步步道
anchor〔'æŋkɚ〕 *v.* 下錨；停泊
unusual〔ʌn'juʒʊəl〕 *adj.* 不尋常的；特別的
sight〔saɪt〕 *n.* 景象
stroll〔strol〕 *v.* 散步；閒逛
along〔ə'lɔŋ〕 *prep.* 沿著　　waterfront〔'wɑtɚ,frʌnt〕 *n.* 水邊
take a break 休息一下　　***in the middle of*** 在～中間

全民英語能力分級檢定測驗

中級英語檢定複試測驗③

寫作能力測驗

本測驗共有兩部份。第一部份為中譯英，第二部份為英文作文。測驗時間為 **40 分鐘**。

一、中譯英（40％）

說明： 請將下列的一段中文翻譯成通順、達意且前後連貫的英文。

　　時間的輪子不停地在轉動。無數的明天變成今天，今天又變成昨天。昨天是今天的殷鑑。如果昨天你失敗了，今天切莫灰心。你必須把你的失敗作為一種教訓，來改正自己，這對你是一種警告或鼓勵。今天是我們唯一能利用的時間，所以我們必須緊緊把握住。明天是希望的來源。如果沒有明天，人將沒有希望。由此可知，明天對我們是多麼地重要啊！

二、英文作文（60％）

說明： 請依下面所提供的文字提示寫一篇英文作文，長度約 120 字（8 至 12 個句子）。作文可以是一個完整的段落，也可以分段。（評分重點包括內容、組織、文法、用字遣詞、標點符號、大小寫。）

提示： 當你感到寂寞時（When I Feel Lonely），你會想到什麼人、事、物呢？請寫一篇文章描述：
　　　寂寞時，你會做什麼事，來排遣你的寂寞呢？

中級英檢寫作練習

口説能力測驗

請在 15 秒內完成並唸出下列自我介紹的句子：

My seat number is （複試座位號碼後 5 碼）, and my registration number is （初試准考證號碼後 5 碼）.

第一段份：朗讀短文

請先利用一分鐘的時間閱讀下面的短文，然後在二分鐘內以正常的速度，清楚正確的讀出下面的短文，閱讀時請不要發出聲音。

There was a knock at the door. It was a small boy, about five years old. Something of his had found its way into my garage, he said, and he wanted it back. Upon opening the garage door, I noticed two additions: a baseball and a broken window with a baseball-sized hole. "How do you suppose this ball got in here?" I asked. Taking one look at the ball, one look at the window and one look at me, the boy exclaimed, "Wow! I must have thrown it right through that hole."

*   *   *

Mother Teresa arrives in Heaven. "Be thou hungry?" God asks. Mother Teresa nods. He serves up some tuna sandwiches. Meanwhile, the sainted woman looks down to see gluttons in Hell devouring steaks, lobsters and wine. The next day God invites her to join him for another meal. Again, it's tuna. Again, she sees the residents of Hell feasting. As another can of tuna is opened the following day, Mother Teresa meekly says, "I am grateful to be here with you as a reward for the pious life I led. But I don't understand. All we eat is tuna and bread while in the other place they eat like kings." "Let's face it," God says with a deep sigh, "for just two people, does it pay to cook?"

第二部份：回答問題

共十題。題目已事先錄音，每題經由耳機播出二次，不印在試卷上。第一至五題，每題回答時間 15 秒；第六至十題，每題回答時間 30 秒。每題播出後，請立即回答。回答時，不一定要用完整的句子，但請在作答時間內儘量的表達。

第三部份：看圖敘述

下面有一張圖片及四個相關的問題，請在一分半鐘內完成作答。作答時，請直接回答，不需將題號及題目唸出。

首先請利用 30 秒的時間看圖及問題。

1. 這可能是什麼地方？
2. 這裡的環境如何？
3. 圖片裡的人在做什麼？
4. 請敘述圖片中人物的穿著以及景物。

請將下列自我介紹的句子再唸一遍：

My seat number is （複試座位號碼後 5 碼）, and my registration number is （初試准考證號碼後 5 碼）.

口說能力測驗解答

第一部份：朗讀短文

請先利用一分鐘的時間閱讀下面二篇短文，閱讀時請不要發出聲音，然後在二分鐘之內以正常的速度，清楚正確的讀出下面的短文。

There was a knock at the door. It was a small boy,

about five years old. Something of his had found its

way into my garage, he said, and he wanted it back.

Upon opening the garage door, I noticed two additions:

a baseball and a broken window with a baseball-sized

hole. "How do you suppose this ball got in here?" I

asked. Taking one look at the ball, one look at the

window and one look at me, the boy exclaimed, "Wow!

I must have thrown it right through that hole."

【註】 knock〔nɑk〕n. 敲門（聲）　　*find one's way into* 進入

garage〔gəˈrɑʒ〕n. 車庫　　*upon + V-ing* 一…就

notice〔ˈnotɪs〕v. 注意到

addition〔əˈdɪʃən〕n. 多餘、額外之物

take one look at 看一眼

exclaim〔ɪkˈsklem〕v. 大聲說；大叫

right〔raɪt〕adv. 正好

Mother Teresa arrives in Heaven. "Be thou hungry?" God asks. Mother Teresa nods. He serves up some tuna sandwiches. Meanwhile, the sainted woman looks down to see gluttons in Hell devouring steaks, lobsters and wine. The next day God invites her to join him for another meal. Again, it's tuna. Again, she sees the residents of Hell feasting. As another can of tuna is opened the following day, Mother Teresa meekly says, "I am grateful to be here with you as a reward for the pious life I led. But I don't understand. All we eat is tuna and bread while in the other place they eat like kings." "Let's face it," God says with a deep sigh, "for just two people, does it pay to cook?"

【註】 Mother〔ˈmʌðɚ〕*n.* 女修道院院長　　Teresa〔təˈrisə〕*n.* 德蕾莎
Mother Teresa 德蕾莎修女　　heaven〔ˈhɛvən〕*n.* 天堂
thou〔ðaʊ〕*pron.*【古英文】你(= you)
Be thou hungry? 你會餓嗎(= Are you hungry?)
nod〔nɑd〕*v.* 點頭　　*serve up* 把⋯端上餐桌
tuna〔ˈtunə〕*n.* 鮪魚　　meanwhile〔ˈminˌhwaɪl〕*adv.* 同時
sainted〔ˈsentɪd〕*adj.* 列入聖徒的；道德崇高的；被召入天國的
glutton〔ˈglʌtn̩〕*n.* 貪吃者　　hell〔hɛl〕*n.* 地獄
devour〔dɪˈvaʊr〕*v.* 狼吞虎嚥地吃　　steak〔stek〕*n.* 牛排
lobster〔ˈlɑbstɚ〕*n.* 龍蝦　　wine〔waɪn〕*n.* 葡萄酒
meal〔mil〕*n.* 一餐　　resident〔ˈrɛzədənt〕*n.* 居民
feast〔fist〕*v.* 大吃；飽餐　　can〔kæn〕*n.* 罐子
meekly〔ˈmiklɪ〕*adv.* 溫順地　　grateful〔ˈgretfəl〕*adj.* 感激的
reward〔rɪˈwɔrd〕*n.* 報酬 <for>

pious〔'paɪəs〕*adj.* 虔誠的；值得稱讚的

lead〔lid〕*v.* 過著（…生活）　　while〔hwaɪl〕*conj.* 然而

face it 面對現實　　sigh〔saɪ〕*n.* 嘆息

pay〔pe〕*v.* 值得；划得來

第二部份：回答問題

Question 1： *How was your last weekend? What did you do?*

Answer： I had a great weekend.

I slept in till noon last Saturday.

I went out with friends in the afternoon.

On Sunday we had a family reunion at home.

All my aunts, uncles and cousins came to my house.

We ate and chatted and sang karaoke together.

sleep in 睡得晚　　reunion〔ri'junjən〕*n.* 團圓；聚會

cousin〔'kʌzn̩〕*n.* 表（堂）兄弟姊妹

chat〔tʃæt〕*v.* 聊天　　karaoke〔ˌkɑrɑ'oke〕*n.* 卡拉 OK

Question 2： *Have you ever been to a hot spring? How did you like it?*

Answer： Yes, I have many times.

I think hot springs are heavenly.

Hot springs are my idea of paradise.

The hot water relaxes my muscles.

The hot spring soothes my soul.

I always come out feeling like a new person.

spring〔sprɪŋ〕*n.* 泉水　　*hot spring* 溫泉

heavenly〔'hɛvənlɪ〕*adj.* 天堂般的；極好的

my idea of 我所認為的　　paradise〔'pærəˌdaɪs〕*n.* 天堂；樂園

> relax〔rɪ'læks〕v. 放鬆　　muscle〔'mʌsḷ〕n. 肌肉
> soothe〔suð〕v. 撫慰；緩和　　soul〔sol〕n. 靈魂

Question 3 : *Do you like comic books? Why or why not?*

Answer : I enjoy comics very much.

I used to collect them as a kid.

They are so humorous and amusing.

The cartoon drawings are cute.

The captions are clever.

Comic books are a lot of fun.

> *comic books*　漫畫書（＝*comics*）
> humorous〔'hjumərəs〕*adj.* 幽默的
> amusing〔ə'mjuzɪŋ〕*adj.* 有趣的　　cartoon〔kɑr'tun〕*n.* 卡通
> drawing〔'drɔ·ɪŋ〕*n.* 圖畫　　cute〔kjut〕*adj.* 可愛的
> caption〔'kæpʃən〕*n.* （照片、插圖的）文字說明
> *be a lot of fun*　很有趣

Question 4 : *When would you normally take a shower and when would you take a bath?*

Answer : I normally take a shower every day.

It's fast, convenient and feels good.

It refreshes me and picks me up.

I usually take a bath on weekends.

I have more time to sit and soak.

I love to read or stretch out in the tub.

> normally〔'nɔrmḷɪ〕*adv.* 通常（＝*usually*）
> *take a shower*　淋浴　　*take a bath*　洗澡；泡澡
> feel〔fil〕*v.* 使人感覺
> refresh〔rɪ'frɛʃ〕*v.* 使提神；使恢復精神（＝*pick sb. up*）

soak〔sok〕*v.* 浸泡　　***stretch out*** 伸展四肢
tub〔tʌb〕*n.* 浴缸（=*bathtub*）

Question 5：*Did you ever tell a white lie? Why or why not?*

Answer：Yes, I did.

Sometimes it is unavoidable.

Sometimes the truth is too painful.

White lies can protect the innocent.

They can comfort a naïve child.

They can console a broken heart.

tell a lie 說謊　　***white lie*** 善意的謊言
unavoidable〔͵ʌnə'vɔɪdəbḷ〕*adj.* 無法避免的
painful〔'penfəl〕*adj.* 痛苦的　　innocent〔'ɪnəsn̩t〕*adj.* 無辜的
the innocent 無辜的人（=*innocent people*）
comfort〔'kʌmfɚt〕*v.* 安慰　　naïve〔nɑ'iv〕*adj.* 天真的
console〔kən'sol〕*v.* 安慰（=*comfort*）

Question 6：*What are your favorite colors and how do you feel about them?*

Answer：I really like sky blue.

It's so cool and relaxing.

It makes me feel like a cloud floating high.

Besides, red really fires me up.

It's romantic and passionate.

It makes me want to fall in love.

cool〔kul〕*adj.* 涼爽的　　relaxing〔rɪ'læksɪŋ〕*adj.* 令人放鬆的
float〔flot〕*v.* 飄浮　　high〔haɪ〕*adv.* 高高地
fire sb. up 使某人激動（=*make sb. enthusiastic*）
romantic〔ro'mæntɪk〕*adj.* 浪漫的

passionate〔'pæʃənɪt〕*adj.* 熱情的　　***fall in love*** 戀愛

Question 7 : *Is learning English easier or more difficult than you expected? Please explain*.

Answer : It's a little of both.

It's easier to comprehend.

It's more difficult to communicate.

At first, I was discouraged by my slow progress.

Then, I became determined to persevere.

Now, I'm confident I'll master English.

comprehend〔ˌkɑmprɪ'hɛnd〕*v.* 理解
discourage〔dɪ'skɝɪdʒ〕*v.* 使氣餒
progress〔'prɑgrɛs〕*n.* 進步
determined〔dɪ'tɝmɪnd〕*adj.* 堅決的
persevere〔ˌpɝsə'vɪr〕*v.* 堅忍；不屈不撓
confident〔'kɑnfədənt〕*adj.* 有信心的
master〔'mæstɚ〕*v.* 精通

Question 8 : *Do you prefer reading a good novel or watching a good movie? Please explain*.

Answer : I prefer a good novel.

I like to use my imagination.

I like to create a picture in my mind.

I can enjoy it at my own pace.

I can keep it and re-read it many times.

It offers me more than a movie does.

imagination〔ˌɪmædʒə'neʃən〕*n.* 想像力
create〔krɪ'et〕*v.* 創造　　pace〔pes〕*n.* 步調
time〔taɪm〕*n.* 次數　　offer〔'ɔfɚ〕*v.* 提供

Question 9　: *What do you usually do to get out of a bad mood?*

Answer　: I usually get up and take action.

I don't dwell on negative thoughts.

I turn on some music to forget the bad feelings.

Sometimes I try physical exercise.

I also seek out a good friend.

Talking about it will make me feel better.

get out of　擺脫　　　mood〔mud〕*n.* 心情
get up　站起來　　*take action*　採取行動
dwell on　老是想著　　negative〔'nɛgətɪv〕*adj.* 負面的
turn on　打開　　physical〔'fɪzɪkl̩〕*adj.* 身體的
seek out　找出

Question 10　: *If you could be an expert in one certain field, or a Jack-of-all-trades, which would you choose? Please explain.*

Answer　: I'd choose to be a Jack-of-all-trades.

I'd rather be well-rounded.

I'd rather know a little bit about a lot.

I'd like lots of general knowledge.

That would give me more to talk about with people.

That would help me more with the many challenges
　of life.

expert〔'ɛkspɝt〕*n.* 專家　　certain〔'sɝtn̩〕*adj.* 某個
field〔fild〕*n.* 領域
a Jack-of-all-trades　萬事通；博而不精者
would rather　寧願
well-rounded〔'wɛl'raʊndɪd〕*adj.* 通才的；多才多藝的
general〔'dʒɛnərəl〕*adj.* 一般的；普遍的
challenge〔'tʃælɪndʒ〕*n.* 挑戰

第三部份：看圖敘述

1. This is a picture of a village square.

2. It is a small village in Europe and the square is in front of a church and a stage has been set up before the bell tower.

3. The people in the picture are celebrating a special day.

4 Some people are wearing traditional clothes and doing a traditional dance on the stage. Spectators gathered around the stage and are watching the show happily. It is a nice day and everyone is enjoying the festival.

【註】 village〔'vɪlɪdʒ〕 *n.* 鄉村 　　square〔skwɛr〕 *n.* 廣場
stage〔stedʒ〕 *n.* 舞台 　 ***set up*** 設立
bell tower 鐘樓 　　celebrate〔'sɛlə,bret〕 *v.* 慶祝
traditional〔trə'dɪʃənḷ〕 *adj.* 傳統的 　 ***do a dance*** 跳一個舞
spectator〔'spɛktetɚ〕 *n.* 觀眾
festival〔'fɛstəvḷ〕 *n.* 節日；節慶

全民英語能力分級檢定測驗

中級英語檢定複試測驗④

寫作能力測驗

本測驗共有兩部份。第一部份為中譯英，第二部份為英文作文。測驗時間為 **40 分鐘**。

一、中譯英（40 %）

說明：　請將下列的一段中文翻譯成通順、達意且前後連貫的英文。

　　　　一談到出國旅遊，日本似乎是每個人優先考慮的國家。去年春天，我就去了日本，那裡到處都是盛開的櫻花。在他們的街道或者是公園裡，都找不到垃圾。我猜想，東京一定是世界上最乾淨的都市之一。我此行另外一件值得注意的事情，就是有關日本人自身的問題。他們的公德心和禮貌真是令人欽佩。跟日本人比起來，我們的國家還有很多地方要改進。

二、英文作文（60 %）

說明：　請依下面所提供的文字提示寫一篇英文作文，長度約 120 字（8 至 12
　　　　個句子）。作文可以是一個完整的段落，也可以分段。（評分重點包
　　　　括內容、組織、文法、用字遣詞、標點符號、大小寫。）

提示：　俗話說：助人為快樂之本。請寫一篇文章描述：

　　　　⑴ 你曾經幫助過別人嗎（An Experience of Helping Others）？

　　　　⑵ 助人之後你有什麼樣的感受呢？

中級英檢寫作練習

口說能力測驗

請在 15 秒內完成並唸出下列自我介紹的句子：

My seat number is （複試座位號碼後 5 碼）, and my registration number is （初試准考證號碼後 5 碼）.

第一段份：朗讀短文

請先利用一分鐘的時間閱讀下面的短文，然後在二分鐘內以正常的速度，清楚正確的讀出下面的短文，閱讀時請不要發出聲音。

Very early one morning, my father came into my room. He shook me awake. "Come on, Karen," he said. "Get the sleep out of your eyes. I want to show you something." I followed him downstairs. It was early and still dark outside. Even the seagulls were still asleep. We drove along the sandy road to the beach and climbed out of the car. The ocean looked beautiful in the early gray light. It was full of tiny sea animals called plankton. They shone like stars as the waves hit the shore. I will never forget that dawn when the beach sparkled like a dream.

*　　　　　　　*　　　　　　　*

Birds are outstanding air travelers. Some kinds fly thousands of miles yearly, as they migrate from north to south and back again. A few kinds of bats also migrate, feeding on insects in the air as they travel. Locusts, which are similar to grasshoppers, sometimes fly in great swarms. Some swarms are so great as to blot out the sun for hours. They move across the sky like huge black clouds. Honeybees travel by air to carry nectar and pollen from flowers to their hive. Think how difficult their work would be if bees had to crawl, fully loaded, all the way back to their hives.

第二部份：回答問題

共十題。題目已事先錄音，每題經由耳機播出二次，不印在試卷上。第一至五題，每題回答時間 15 秒；第六至十題，每題回答時間 30 秒。每題播出後，請立即回答。回答時，不一定要用完整的句子，但請在作答時間內儘量的表達。

第三部份：看圖敘述

下面有一張圖片及四個相關的問題，請在一分半鐘內完成作答。作答時，請直接回答，不需將題號及題目唸出。

首先請利用 30 秒的時間看圖及問題。

1. 這可能是什麼地方？
2. 這裡的環境如何？
3. 圖片裡的人在做什麼？
4. 請敘述圖片中人物的活動以及景物。

請將下列自我介紹的句子再唸一遍：

My seat number is（複試座位號碼後 5 碼）, and my registration number is（初試准考證號碼後 5 碼）.

口說能力測驗解答

第一部份：朗讀短文

請先利用一分鐘的時間閱讀下面二篇短文，閱讀時請不要發出聲音，然後在二分鐘之內以正常的速度，清楚正確的讀出下面的短文。

Very early one morning, my father came into my room. He shook me awake. "Come on, Karen," he said. "Get the sleep out of your eyes. I want to show you something." I followed him downstairs. It was early and still dark outside. Even the seagulls were still asleep. We drove along the sandy road to the beach and climbed out of the car. The ocean looked beautiful in the early gray light. It was full of tiny sea animals called plankton. They shone like stars as the waves hit the shore. I will never forget that dawn when the beach sparkled like a dream.

【註】 *shake sb. awake* 把某人搖醒　　sleep〔slip〕n. 睡意
downstairs〔'daun'stɛrz〕adv. 到樓下
seagull〔'si͵gʌl〕n. 海鷗　　asleep〔ə'slip〕adj. 睡著的
sandy〔'sændɪ〕adj. 多沙的　　gray〔gre〕adj. 灰色的
tiny〔'taɪnɪ〕adj. 微小的　　plankton〔'plæŋktən〕n. 浮游生物
shine〔ʃaɪn〕v. 發光（三態變化為：shine-shone-shone）
shore〔ʃor〕n. 海岸　　dawn〔dɔn〕n. 黎明
sparkle〔'spɑrk!〕v. 發光

　　Birds are outstanding air travelers.　Some kinds fly thousands
of miles yearly, as they migrate from north to south and back
again.　A few kinds of bats also migrate, feeding on insects in
the air as they travel.　Locusts, which are similar to grasshoppers,
sometimes fly in great swarms.　Some swarms are so great as to
blot out the sun for hours.　They move across the sky like huge
black clouds.　Honeybees travel by air to carry nectar and pollen
from flowers to their hive.　Think how difficult their work
would be if bees had to crawl, fully loaded, all the way back to
their hives.

【註】 outstanding〔ˈaʊtˈstændɪŋ〕*adj.* 傑出的
　　　　yearly〔ˈjɪrlɪ〕*adv.* 每年　　migrate〔ˈmaɪgret〕*v.* 遷移
　　　　feed on 以～爲食　　insect〔ˈɪnˌsɛkt〕*n.* 昆蟲
　　　　in the air 在空中　　travel〔ˈtrævl̩〕*v.* 行進；前進
　　　　locust〔ˈlokəst〕*n.* 蝗蟲　　grasshopper〔ˈgræsˌhapɚ〕*n.* 蚱蜢
　　　　swarm〔swɔrm〕*n.* 一群（昆蟲）　　***blot out*** 遮蔽
　　　　huge〔hjudʒ〕*adj.* 巨大的
　　　　honeybee〔ˈhʌnɪˌbi〕*n.* 蜜蜂（＝*bee*）
　　　　travel by air 飛行　　nectar〔ˈnɛktɚ〕*n.* 花蜜
　　　　pollen〔ˈpɑlən〕*n.* 花粉　　hive〔haɪv〕*n.* 蜂窩（＝*beehive*）
　　　　crawl〔krɔl〕*v.* 爬行　　　　loaded〔ˈlodɪd〕*adj.* 裝滿東西的

第二部份：回答問題

Question 1：*Have you ever visited any kind of exhibition?*

Answer：Sure, I've been to a few.

I've been to book fairs.

I've enjoyed computer shows.

There are always lots of people crowding the shows.

The prices are usually lower with better discounts.

Sometimes there are also some free bonuses.

exhibition〔͵ɛksə'bɪʃən〕*n.* 展覽（= *fair*）
have been to 曾經去過　　***book fair*** 書展
show〔ʃo〕*n.* 展示會　　crowd〔kraʊd〕*v.* 使擠滿
discount〔'dɪskaʊnt〕*n.* 折扣　　free〔fri〕*adj.* 免費的
bonus〔'bonəs〕*n.* 額外的贈品

Question 2：*Do you like to wear jeans or not? Please explain.*

Answer：I enjoy wearing jeans.

They are convenient to wear.

They feel so comfortable.

I like casual wear.

Jeans are the most suitable for me.

Tight or loose, jeans are cool.

jeans〔dʒinz〕*n. pl.* 牛仔褲　　feel〔fil〕*adj.* 使人感覺
casual〔'kæʒʊəl〕*adj.* 休閒的；輕便的　　wear〔wɛr〕*n.* …服裝
casual wear 便服　　suitable〔'sutəbl̩〕*adj.* 適合的
tight〔taɪt〕*adj.* 緊的　　loose〔lus〕*adj.* 寬鬆的
cool〔kul〕*adj.* 很酷的；很棒的

Question 3 : *Have you ever given away your seat on a bus*
or a train?

Answer : Yes, I have many times.

I feel it's my duty.

I'm happy to help someone out.

It feels great to be nice.

The elderly and young kids deserve it.

The handicapped and pregnant women need help too.

give away one's seat 讓座　　duty〔'djutɪ〕*n.* 義務；責任
help sb. out 幫助某人　　elderly〔'ɛldə·lɪ〕*adj.* 年長的
deserve〔dɪ'zɝv〕*v.* 應得
handicapped〔'hændɪ‚kæpt〕*adj.* 殘障的
pregnant〔'prɛgnənt〕*adj.* 懷孕的

Question 4 : *What kind of person is your English teacher?*

Answer : My English teacher is very dedicated.

She is very professional.

She cares about every student, too.

She is demanding yet patient.

She is an expert teacher.

I hope I can become as good as she is.

dedicated〔'dɛdə‚ketɪd〕*adj.* 投入的（= *devoted*）
professional〔prə'fɛʃən!〕*adj.* 專業的
demanding〔dɪ'mændɪŋ〕*adj.* 苛求的；要求多的
expert〔'ɛkspɝt〕*adj.* 熟練的；專業的

Question 5： *What do you do to stay healthy?*

Answer： I try to eat a balanced diet.

I try to eat lots of fruit and vegetables.

I try to avoid sweets and junk food.

Sometimes I exercise.

I play ball or go jogging.

Besides, I try to get enough sleep.

stay healthy 保持健康　balanced〔'bælənst〕*adj.* 均衡的
diet〔'daɪət〕*n.* 飲食　avoid〔ə'vɔɪd〕*v.* 避免
sweets〔swits〕*n. pl.* 甜食　*junk food* 垃圾食物
jog〔dʒɑg〕*n.* 慢跑

Question 6： *If you need to improve on a certain subject, would you consider hiring a tutor or going to a cram school?*

Answer： I'd attend a cram school.

The teachers are more experienced.

The facilities are usually better.

Tutors are too expensive.

Tutors are not always reliable.

Cram schools guarantee good results.

improve〔ɪm'pruv〕*v.* 改善 <*on*>　certain〔'sɝtn̩〕*adj.* 某個
consider〔kən'sɪdɚ〕*v.* 考慮　hire〔haɪr〕*v.* 雇用
tutor〔'tjutɚ〕*n.* 家敎　*cram school* 補習班
attend〔ə'tɛnd〕*v.* 上（學）　facilities〔fə'sɪlətɪz〕*n. pl.* 設施
reliable〔rɪ'laɪəbl̩〕*adj.* 可靠的
guarantee〔ˌgærən'ti〕*v.* 保證
results〔rɪ'zʌlts〕*n. pl.* 成果；（考試）成績

Question 7 : *Suppose your family will soon have a newborn baby. Would you prefer it to be a boy or a girl?*

Answer : My family wouldn't care.

It wouldn't matter to us.

Either a boy or a girl would be great.

We'd welcome a boy.

We'd love to have a girl.

Having a healthy child is what counts.

suppose〔sə'poz〕*v.* 假定;假設

newborn〔'nju,bɔrn〕*adj.* 新生的　　prefer〔prɪ'fɝ〕*v.* 比較喜歡

matter〔'mætɚ〕*v.* 重要;有關係　　count〔kaʊnt〕*v.* 重要

Question 8 : *Are you an early bird or a night owl? Please explain*.

Answer : I'm a night owl for sure.

I enjoy staying up late.

I seldom go to bed early.

Nighttime is peaceful and quiet.

I can do my homework undisturbed.

It helps me study efficiently.

an early bird 早睡早起的人　　owl〔aʊl〕*n.* 貓頭鷹

a night owl 夜貓子　　*for sure* 一定地;確實地

stay up 熬夜　　nighttime〔'naɪt,taɪm〕*n.* 夜晚

peaceful〔'pisfəl〕*adj.* 寧靜的

undisturbed〔,ʌndɪ'stɝbd〕*adj.* 不受打擾的

efficiently〔ə'fɪʃəntlɪ〕*adv.* 有效率地

Question 9 : *When you are riding on the MRT, a bus or a train, what do you usually do?*

Answer : I usually like to read.

Sometimes I run through my notes.

Sometimes I just sit and relax.

Watching people is interesting.

Looking out the window is fun too.

I like taking public transportation.

run through 瀏覽　　notes〔nots〕*n. pl.* 筆記

look out (*of*)　從…往外看

look out (*of*) *the window*　朝窗外看　　fun〔fʌn〕*adj.* 有趣的

transportation〔͵trænspɚ'teʃən〕*n.* 交通；運輸

public transportation　大衆運輸工具

Question 10 : *Do you think English is an interesting subject? Why or why not?*

Answer : Yes, I think English is interesting.

It's a useful language.

Conversation is what I like most.

Memorizing vocabulary is hard work.

Grammar and reading are a lot more difficult.

But I still enjoy the challenge.

vocabulary〔və'kæbjə͵lɛrɪ〕*n.* 字彙

memorize〔'mɛmə͵raɪz〕*v.* 記憶；背誦

grammar〔'græmɚ〕*n.* 文法　　enjoy〔ɪn'dʒɔɪ〕*v.* 喜歡

challenge〔'tʃælɪndʒ〕*n.* 挑戰

第三部份：看圖敘述

1. This is a picture of a young boy in a room.

2. The room is sparsely furnished. There is a television on a TV stand and a tall floor lamp in the corner beside the window.

3. The boy is sitting on the floor, watching a cartoon, after having finished a snack.

4. It's a beautiful day since the sun is shining through the window. The boy is relaxing in front of the TV after a long day in school. He is enjoying his favorite cartoon. However, he is sitting too close to the TV, which is a bad habit and could damage his eyesight.

【註】 sparsely〔'spɑrslɪ〕*adv.* 稀疏地；稀少地
furnish〔'fɜnɪʃ〕*v.* 裝備家具　　stand〔stænd〕*n.* …台；…架
floor lamp 落地燈　　corner〔'kɔrnɚ〕*n.* 角落
finish〔'fɪnɪʃ〕*v.* 吃完　　snack〔snæk〕*n.* 點心
eyesight〔'aɪ,saɪt〕*n.* 視力

全民英語能力分級檢定測驗

中級英語檢定複試測驗⑤

寫作能力測驗

本測驗共有兩部份。第一部份為中譯英，第二部份為英文作文。測驗時間為**40 分鐘**。

一、中譯英（40 %）

說明： 請將下列的一段中文翻譯成通順、達意且前後連貫的英文。

　　我怕死飛行了。我從來沒有坐過飛機，而我相信我未來也絕對不會去坐。然而，我喜歡去機場，看著那裡形形色色的人。在今年新年期間，我帶著一大包爆米花，和許多面紙，到桃園國際機場去。我走到入境區，坐在前排，看到許多家人團聚的場面。那些畫面是如此感人，以致於我的眼睛都沒有乾過。

二、英文作文（60 %）

說明： 請依下面所提供的文字提示寫一篇英文作文，長度約 120 字（8 至 12 個句子）。作文可以是一個完整的段落，也可以分段。（評分重點包括內容、組織、文法、用字遣詞、標點符號、大小寫。）

提示： 身體健康固然重要，但心理健康也是很重要的（The Importance of Mental Health）。請寫一篇文章說明：(1) 要如何保持心理健康呢？(2) 心理健康有什麼重大的影響呢？

中級英檢寫作練習

口說能力測驗

請在 15 秒內完成並唸出下列自我介紹的句子：

My seat number is （複試座位號碼後 5 碼）, and my registration number is （初試准考證號碼後 5 碼）.

第一段份：朗讀短文

請先利用一分鐘的時間閱讀下面的短文，然後在二分鐘內以正常的速度，清楚正確的讀出下面的短文，閱讀時請不要發出聲音。

What a great difference there is between a bark and a growl! When a dog barks, he throws his head high. A bark is not a war cry. But when a dog growls, he lowers his head. A growl often means he is ready to fight. The dog must guard his throat when he fights other animals. If a dog comes barking to meet you, you are in no danger. But what if he comes towards you growling and with his head lowered? Then you should look out for trouble! Stand still. Put your hands on your chest. If you do this, not one dog in ten will bite you. Do not hit the dog or turn and run.

*　　　　　　*　　　　　　*

In every large city, there are neighborhoods where immigrants keep their languages and traditions alive. In New York City there is "Little Italy." Many people there speak Italian and celebrate festivals from the old country. In Miami's "Little Havana," Cuban culture is very evident, and you can hear Spanish on the street and see shop windows full of advertisements in Spanish. Many cities have a neighborhood called Chinatown. There are many Chinese restaurants and businesses in these neighborhoods. People are proud of their customs and traditions. They keep them alive in their neighborhoods.

第二部份：回答問題

共十題。題目已事先錄音，每題經由耳機播出二次，不印在試卷上。第一至五題，每題回答時間 15 秒；第六至十題，每題回答時間 30 秒。每題播出後，請立即回答。回答時，不一定要用完整的句子，但請在作答時間內儘量的表達。

第三部份：看圖敘述

下面有一張圖片及四個相關的問題，請在一分半鐘內完成作答。作答時，請直接回答，不需將題號及題目唸出。

首先請利用 30 秒的時間看圖及問題。

1. 這是什麼地方？
2. 這裡的環境如何？
3. 圖裡的人在做什麼？
4. 請敘述圖片中可能發生的事情和結果。

請將下列自我介紹的句子再唸一遍：

My seat number is （複試座位號碼後 5 碼）, and my registration number is （初試准考證號碼後 5 碼）.

口說能力測驗解答

第一部份：朗讀短文

請先利用一分鐘的時間閱讀下面二篇短文，閱讀時請不要發出聲音，然後在二分鐘之內以正常的速度，清楚正確的讀出下面的短文。

What a great difference there is between a bark and a growl! When a dog barks, he throws his head high. A bark is not a war cry. But when a dog growls, he lowers his head. A growl often means he is ready to fight. The dog must guard his throat when he fights other animals. If a dog comes barking to meet you, you are in no danger. But what if he comes towards you growling and with his head lowered? Then you should look out for trouble! Stand still. Put your hands on your chest. If you do this, not one dog in ten will bite you. Do not hit the dog or turn and run.

【註】 bark〔bɑrk〕n. v.（狗）吠叫　　growl〔graʊl〕n. v. 咆哮；吼叫
throw〔θro〕v.（猛烈地）動（身體的某個部位）
throw one's head high 猛然把頭抬高
war cry 作戰時戰士的吶喊
lower〔'loɚ〕v. 降低　　guard〔gɑrd〕v. 保護
throat〔θrot〕n. 喉嚨　　meet〔mit〕v. 面對
what if 如果…該怎麼辦　　***look out for*** 小心；注意
still〔stɪl〕adj. 靜止的；不動的　　chest〔tʃɛst〕n. 胸部

In every large city, there are neighborhoods where immigrants keep their languages and traditions alive. In New York City there is "Little Italy." Many people there speak Italian and celebrate festivals from the old country. In Miami's "Little Havana," Cuban culture is very evident, and you can hear Spanish on the street and see shop windows full of advertisements in Spanish. Many cities have a neighborhood called Chinatown. There are many Chinese restaurants and businesses in these neighborhoods. People are proud of their customs and traditions. They keep them alive in their neighborhoods.

【註】 neighborhood〔'nebɚ,hʊd〕*n.* 鄰近地區;社區
immigrant〔'ɪməgrənt〕*n.* (移入的)移民
tradition〔trə'dɪʃən〕*n.* 傳統
alive〔ə'laɪv〕*adj.* 活著的;存在的
festival〔'fɛstəvl〕*n.* 節慶　　old〔old〕*adj.* 從前的
Miami〔maɪ'æmɪ〕*n.* 邁阿密
Havana〔hə'vænə〕*n.* 哈瓦那(古巴首都)
Cuban〔'kjubən〕*adj.* 古巴的
evident〔'ɛvədənt〕*adj.* 明顯的　　***be full of*** 充滿了
advertisement〔,ædvɚ'taɪzmənt〕*n.* 廣告
business〔'bɪznɪs〕*n.* 生意;商店;公司

第二部份：回答問題

Question 1：*Are you a superstitious person? Why or why not?*

Answer：I'm not superstitious.

I don't believe all that stuff.

I believe people decide their own fate.

Sometimes I think superstitions are interesting.

They're fun to talk about.

But taboos and omens are for the birds.

superstitious〔͵supɚ'stɪʃəs〕*adj.* 迷信的　　　stuff〔stʌf〕*n.* 東西
fate〔fet〕*n.* 命運　　　superstition〔͵supɚ'stɪʃən〕*n.* 迷信
fun〔fʌn〕*adj.* 有趣的　　　taboo〔tə'bu〕*n.* 禁忌
omen〔'omən〕*n.* 預兆　　*for the birds* 無用的；無聊的

Question 2：*Every person has his own fears. What do you fear most? Please give one or two examples.*

Answer：I'm afraid of big tests.

I hate lots of pressure.

I worry about making mistakes.

Besides, I am scared of snakes.

I recoil and always feel breathless at the sight of one.

It always makes my flesh crawl.

fear〔fɪr〕*n. v.* 恐懼　　　give〔gɪv〕*v.* 提供；說
pressure〔'prɛʃɚ〕*n.* 壓力
be scared of 害怕（= *be afraid of*）　　　snake〔snek〕*n.* 蛇
recoil〔rɪ'kɔɪl〕*v.* 退縮　　　breathless〔'brɛθlɪs〕*adj.* 屏息的
at the sight of 一看到　　　flesh〔flɛʃ〕*n.*（身體的）肌膚
crawl〔krɔl〕*v.* 爬行；毛骨悚然
make one's flesh crawl 使人毛骨悚然（= *make one's flesh creep*）

Question 3： *What is one shortcoming or weakness you'd like to change about yourself?*

Answer： I think failing to concentrate is my shortcoming.

I tire out and lose focus very easily.

I wish I were more energetic and attentive.

I must exercise more to develop my strength.

I want to lengthen my attention span.

When tired, I can either take a nap or have some coffee to pick me up.

shortcoming (ˈʃɔrt͵kʌmɪŋ) *n.* 缺點 (= *weakness*)

fail to V. 未能… concentrate (ˈkɑnsn͵tret) *v.* 專心

tire out 精疲力竭 focus (ˈfokəs) *n.* 焦點；中心；注意力

energetic (͵ɛnɚˈdʒɛtɪk) *adj.* 精力充沛的

attentive (əˈtɛntɪv) *adj.* 專心的；注意的

strength (strɛŋθ) *n.* 力量；體力 lengthen (ˈlɛŋθən) *v.* 延長

attention span 注意力集中的時間 nap (næp) *n.* 小睡

take a nap 小睡片刻 have (hæv) *v.* 喝

pick sb. up 使某人恢復精神

Question 4： *How did you do on your last grade report?*

Answer： I did pretty well.

I passed every subject.

I made considerable progress.

I improved in every class.

My scores all went up.

My average climbed three points.

do (du) *v.* 表現 *grade report* 成績單 *do well* 考得好

considerable (kənˈsɪdərəbl̩) *adj.* 相當大的

progress (ˈprɑgrɛs) *n.* 進步 improve (ɪmˈpruv) *v.* 改善

score〔skor〕*n.* 分數　　***go up*** 上升
average〔'ævərɪdʒ〕*n.* 平均　　climb〔klaɪm〕*v.* 上升
point〔pɔɪnt〕*n.* 點；分數

Question 5 ： *What's the most difficult thing about studying English for you? Please explain.*

Answer ： Conversation is the toughest part for me.

Speaking clearly is no picnic.

Pronunciation is also a challenge.

I'm afraid to make mistakes.

I get nervous and frustrated.

So my confidence level is low.

tough〔tʌf〕*adj.* 困難的　　picnic〔'pɪknɪk〕*n.* 輕鬆簡單的事
pronunciation〔prə,nʌnsɪ'eʃən〕*n.* 發音
nervous〔'nɝvəs〕*adj.* 緊張的
frustrated〔'frʌstretɪd〕*adj.* 受挫的
confidence〔'kɑnfədəns〕*n.* 信心；自信　　level〔'lɛvl̩〕*n.* 程度

Question 6 ： *Have you ever spent a night in the hospital? Please explain.*

Answer ： No, I never have.

Luckily, I've been healthy.

But my brother has once.

He was hospitalized because of pneumonia.

And my parents had to accompany him overnight.

This made me fully aware of the importance of health.

luckily〔'lʌkɪlɪ〕*adv.* 幸運地
hospitalize〔'hɑspɪtl̩,aɪz〕*v.* 使住院
pneumonia〔nju'monjə〕*n.* 肺炎
accompany〔ə'kʌmpənɪ〕*v.* 陪伴

overnight〔'ovɚ'naɪt〕*adv.* 整夜地
aware〔ə'wɛr〕*adj.* 知道的;察覺到的 *< of >*

Question 7 : *What are some major environmental problems in your country? Please explain.*

Answer : I think air pollution is the worst one.

Vehicle emissions and ignorant people are to blame.

Industrial pollution is choking our lungs.

Land abuse is a serious problem too.

We are overdeveloping land.

Land exploitation is killing nature.

vehicle〔'viɪkl̩〕*n.* 車輛　　emission〔ɪ'mɪʃən〕*n.* (汽車的) 排氣
ignorant〔'ɪgnərənt〕*adj.* 無知的
be to blame 該受責備;就是原因
industrial〔ɪn'dʌstrɪəl〕*adj.* 工業的　　choke〔tʃok〕*v.* 使窒息
lung〔lʌŋ〕*n.* 肺　　abuse〔ə'bjus〕*n.* 濫用
exploitation〔ˌɛksplɔɪ'teʃən〕*n.* 開發
kill〔kɪl〕*v.* 破壞　　nature〔'netʃɚ〕*n.* 大自然

Question 8 : *If you could change one thing about your appearance, what would it be?*

Answer : I'd like to be taller.

I feel I'm too short.

If I added a few centimeters, I'd have more confidence.

Also, I feel I'm a little fat.

I hope to lose some weight.

I'd like to become fitter and slimmer.

appearance〔ə'pɪrɪəns〕*n.* 外表　　add〔æd〕*v.* 增加
centimeter〔'sɛntəˌmitɚ〕*n.* 公分　　*lose weight* 減重
fit〔fɪt〕*adj.* 健康的　　slim〔slɪm〕*adj.* 苗條的

Question 9 ： *Please tell about one of your happiest moments within the last year*.

Answer ： I'd say New Year's Day was the best.

I went to a huge mall with my friends.

I spent all my red envelope money.

I bought some awesome CD's.

I bought clothes and new shoes.

We saw a movie and had a great meal.

tell about　敘述　　　moment〔'momənt〕*n.* 時刻
envelope〔'ɛnvəˌlop〕*n.* 信封　　*red envelope*　紅包
red envelope money　壓歲錢（= *lucky money*）
awesome〔'ɔsəm〕*adj.* 很棒的　　　meal〔mil〕*n.* 一餐

Question 10 ： *If you could visit one European country, which one would you choose and why?*

Answer ： I'd definitely choose France.

I'd love to tour Paris, the capital of romance.

There is so much to see and do.

The Eiffel Tower and the Louvre are must-sees.

I've always dreamed of walking on the Champs Elysees.

And French cuisine is terrific too.

definitely〔'dɛfənɪtlɪ〕*adv.* 一定　　　tour〔tur〕*v.* 遊覽
capital〔'kæpətḷ〕*n.* 首都
romance〔ro'mæns〕*n.* 羅曼史；浪漫的氣氛
Eiffel Tower〔'aɪfḷ'tauɚ〕*n.* 艾菲爾鐵塔
Louvre〔'luvɚ〕*n.* 羅浮宮
must-see〔'mʌstˌsi〕*n.* 必看的事物
Champs Elysees〔ˌʃãzeli'ze〕*n.* 香舍麗榭大道
cuisine〔kwɪ'zin〕*n.* 菜餚

第三部份：看圖敘述

1. This is a picture of a baseball game.

2. The action is taking place at home plate of a baseball diamond.

3. There are three men at home plate. The batter is swinging his bat powerfully, trying to hit the ball. The catcher is trying to catch the ball. The umpire behind the catcher is carefully observing the action.

4. It is an exciting moment, and all eyes are on the batter and the ball. The action is very fast, so it is difficult to determine the outcome—a hit or a miss. In the background, teammates look on with great interest.

【註】 *home plate* 本壘　diamond〔'daɪmənd〕*n.*（棒球場的）內野
batter〔'bætə〕*n.* 打擊者　swing〔swɪŋ〕*v.* 揮（棒）
bat〔bæt〕*n.* 球棒　powerfully〔'pauəfəlɪ〕*adv.* 強有力地
catcher〔'kætʃə〕*n.* 捕手　umpire〔'ʌmpaɪr〕*n.* 裁判
observe〔əb'zɝv〕*v.* 觀察　determine〔dɪ'tɝmɪn〕*v.* 決定；判定
outcome〔'aut,kʌm〕*n.* 結果　hit〔hɪt〕*n.* 安打
miss〔mɪs〕*n.* 沒有打中　background〔'bæk,graund〕*n.* 背景
teammate〔'tim,met〕*n.* 隊友　*look on* 旁觀
with great interest 非常感興趣地

全民英語能力分級檢定測驗

中級英語檢定複試測驗⑥

寫作能力測驗

本測驗共有兩部份。第一部份爲中譯英，第二部份爲英文作文。測驗時間爲 **40 分鐘**。

一、中譯英（40 %）

說明： 請將下列的一段中文翻譯成通順、達意且前後連貫的英文。

　　去年暑假我在一家便利商店打工。那是我第一次打工。工作很辛苦，但是相當有趣。我不但從工作中學習到很多，還結交了不少好朋友。雖然我離開那份工作已經一年了，但是我和我的同事們還是會經常聚會。我很珍惜我們之間的友誼，以及這兩個月的寶貴工作經驗。

二、英文作文（60 %）

說明： 請依下面所提供的文字提示寫一篇英文作文，長度約 120 字（8 至 12 個句子）。作文可以是一個完整的段落，也可以分段。（評分重點包括內容、組織、文法、用字遣詞、標點符號、大小寫。）

提示： 昨天有場爲你的好友 Sandy 舉行的大型慶生會。你收到了邀請函，也已打算要去。但你臨時有事，無法赴會。現在，請寫封信向 Sandy 致歉（A Letter of Apology），並解釋爲何你昨天未出席她的慶生會。

中級英檢寫作練習

口說能力測驗

請在 15 秒內完成並唸出下列自我介紹的句子：

My seat number is （複試座位號碼後 5 碼）, and my registration number is （初試准考證號碼後 5 碼）.

第一段份：朗讀短文

請先利用一分鐘的時間閱讀下面的短文，然後在二分鐘內以正常的速度，清楚正確的讀出下面的短文，閱讀時請不要發出聲音。

The Lees have moved to a new house in the suburbs. It has four bedrooms, two bathrooms, a living room, a dining room and a large kitchen. Next to the house is a large garage. There is also a big yard in back of the house where the children can play. In the new house, there is enough space for each of them to live comfortably. Mr. Lee has his own study now. Mrs. Lee loves the master bedroom with its own bathroom and also enjoys cooking in the kitchen. Their two sons also have rooms to themselves and no longer have to share one. All of them like the new house very much.

* * *

Susan is one of the nicest people that I have ever known. Not only is she friendly and clever, but she's also generous with her time and always willing to help other people. Whenever I have a problem, I turn to her for help, because I know she'll have some good advice for me. It is really fortunate for me to have such a good friend. I really don't know what I would do without her. And of course I will try to be a good friend to her.

第二部份：回答問題

共十題。題目已事先錄音，每題經由耳機播出二次，不印在試卷上。第一至五題，每題回答時間 15 秒；第六至十題，每題回答時間 30 秒。每題播出後，請立即回答。回答時，不一定要用完整的句子，但請在作答時間內儘量的表達。

第三部份：看圖敘述

下面有一張圖片及四個相關的問題，請在一分半鐘內完成作答。作答時，請直接回答，不需將題號及題目唸出。

首先請利用 30 秒的時間看圖及問題。

1. 這可能是什麼地方？
2. 照片裡的人在做什麼？
3. 你喜歡水果嗎？爲什麼？
4. 請敘述圖片中人物的行爲以及景物。

請將下列自我介紹的句子再唸一遍：

My seat number is （複試座位號碼後 5 碼）, and my registration number is （初試准考證號碼後 5 碼）.

口說能力測驗解答

第一部份：朗讀短文

請先利用一分鐘的時間閱讀下面二篇短文，閱讀時請不要發出聲音，然後在二分鐘之內以正常的速度，清楚正確的讀出下面的短文。

The Lees have moved to a new house in the suburbs. It has four bedrooms, two bathrooms, a living room, a dining room and a large kitchen. Next to the house is a large garage. There is also a big yard in back of the house where the children can play. In the new house, there is enough space for each of them to live comfortably. Mr. Lee has his own study now. Mrs. Lee loves the master bedroom with its own bathroom and also enjoys cooking in the kitchen. Their two sons also have rooms to themselves and no longer have to share one. All of them like the new house very much.

【註】 *the Lees* 李家人　　suburbs〔'sʌbɝbz〕 *n. pl.* 郊區
in the suburbs 在郊區　　*next to* 在⋯旁邊
garage〔gə'rɑʒ〕 *n.* 車庫　　yard〔jɑrd〕 *n.* 院子
space〔spes〕 *n.* 空間　　study〔'stʌdɪ〕 *n.* 書房
master〔'mæstɚ〕 *n.* 主人　*adj.* 主要的
master bedroom 主臥室
have ~ to oneself 擁有自己的～
no longer 不再　　share〔ʃɛr〕 *v.* 分享；共用

Susan is one of the nicest people that I have ever known.

Not only is she friendly and clever, but she's also generous

with her time and always willing to help other people.

Whenever I have a problem, I turn to her for help, because

I know she'll have some good advice for me. It is really

fortunate for me to have such a good friend. I really don't

know what I would do without her. And of course I will

try to be a good friend to her.

【註】 clever〔'klɛvɚ〕adj. 聰明的 (= smart)
　　　generous〔'dʒɛnərəs〕adj. 慷慨的；大方的
　　　willing〔'wɪlɪŋ〕adj. 願意的
　　　turn to** sb. **for help 向某人求助
　　　advice〔əd'vaɪs〕n. 忠告；建議
　　　fortunate〔'fɔrtʃənɪt〕adj. 幸運的 (= lucky)

第二部份：回答問題

Question 1：*Did you eat breakfast at home this morning?*
**　　　　　*Why or why not?***

Answer：I didn't eat breakfast at home this morning.

In fact, I rarely do.

I usually buy breakfast on my way to school or
　wherever I'm going.

Of course, I'd love to have a nice big breakfast at home.

However, I'd be late to school that way.

I guess I'll have to wait until I have graduated.

in fact 事實上　　rarely〔ˈrɛrlɪ〕adv. 很少
big〔bɪg〕adj. 豐盛的　　*that way* 那樣；如此一來
graduate〔ˈgrædʒʊˌet〕v. 畢業

Question 2：*How was your last birthday? Did you do anything*
**　　　　　*special?***

Answer：I usually don't do anything special on birthdays.

But last year, my friends held a surprise party for me.

Almost everyone I knew came.

I got lots of great gifts.

They even baked me a cake by themselves.

This year, I'm holding a birthday party to thank them!

hold〔hold〕*v.* 舉行　　***surprise party*** 驚喜派對

bake〔bek〕*v.* 烤　　***by oneself*** 自行；獨自

Question 3：***Will you be going to the movies anytime soon?***
Why or why not?

Answer：I probably will in a couple of days.

In fact, I usually watch one every few weeks.

I consider it a hobby and use it to relax.

Going to a movie is a very different experience
from watching a DVD at home.

The trailers, the lights, and the big screen make
it so much more exciting.

Plus, there is always popcorn!

go to the movies 看電影（= *go to a movie*）

a couple of 幾個；兩三個

consider〔kən'sɪdə〕*v.* 認為　　hobby〔'hɑbɪ〕*n.* 嗜好

trailer〔'trelə〕*n.* 預告片

screen〔skrin〕*n.* 螢幕；銀幕

plus〔plʌs〕*adv.* 此外；再加上

popcorn〔'pɑp,kɔrn〕*n.* 爆米花

Answer：Going to the movies takes a lot of time.

Tickets are also quite expensive.

Therefore, I rarely go to the movies.

I prefer watching movies on DVD.

That way, I don't have to watch it with noisy people.

I can even skip the scenes I don't like.

noisy 〔'nɔɪzɪ 〕 *adj.* 吵鬧的　　skip 〔 skɪp 〕 *v.* 跳過
scene 〔 sin 〕 *n.* 場景；片段

Question 4 : *When you have free time, do you normally stay
at home or go out?*

Answer : I leave home real early and don't return till
　　　　　it's late.
　　　　In fact, sometimes the only thing I do at home
　　　　　is sleep.
　　　　That's why in my free time, I like to stay at home.

　　　　Sometimes I surf the Web or play video games.
　　　　Other times I play my favorite music very loud.
　　　　It's really relaxing to just stay at home and do
　　　　　what you want.

normally 〔'nɔrmḷɪ 〕 *adv.* 通常 (= *usually*)
real 〔'riəl 〕 *adv.* 真地；非常　　*not…until* 直到~才…
the only thing I do at home is (*to*) *V.* 我在家唯一會做的事就是
free time 空閒時間　　surf 〔 sɜf 〕 *v.* 衝浪；瀏覽 (網路)
the Web 網際網路 (= *the Net* = *the Internet*)
surf the Web 上網　　*video game* 電動

Answer : I like to see and visit different places.

I like to meet all kinds of people.

So when I have free time, I like to go out.

If my whole weekend is free, I like to plan
mini-trips.

If I just have a couple of hours, I usually go
shopping or chat with friends.

Going out always makes me happy, and I never
get tired of it.

meet〔mit〕*v.* 認識　　whole〔hol〕*adj.* 整個 (= *entire*)
mini〔'mɪnɪ〕*adj.* 小型的　　chat〔tʃæt〕*v.* 聊天
get tired of 對…厭倦

Question 5 : *How often do you go to the night market? Why do
you do it?*

Answer : I go to the night market about once a month.

Sometimes I go there to buy things

Most of the time, however, it's for the food.

Night markets have some of the most delicious
food ever.

That's why I only go once a month.

If I went more often, I would be really fat.

night market 夜市　　**most of the time** 大部分時候
ever〔ˈɛvɚ〕 *adv.*【在比較級、最高級之後用以強調】以往；至今

Question 6：*Do you think you'll attend the university of your choice? Why or why not?*

Answer：Everyone wants to get into the best universities.
To achieve that goal, we must work hard and
　be diligent.
We also need some good luck.

As long as people persevere, they can do anything
　they want.
So I can't say if I'll get into the university of my
　choice right now.
It all depends on if I can push myself to keep
　going or not.

attend〔əˈtɛnd〕 *v.* 上（學）；就讀
of one's choice 自己挑選的
achieve〔əˈtʃiv〕 *v.* 達成　　goal〔gol〕 *n.* 目標
work hard 努力　　diligent〔ˈdɪlədʒənt〕 *adj.* 勤勉的
as long as 只要
persevere〔ˌpɝsəˈvɪr〕 *v.* 堅忍；不屈不撓
depend on 依賴；取決於；視～而定
push〔pʊʃ〕 *v.* 驅策
keep going 繼續走下去；堅持下去（＝*persevere*）

Question 7 : *What can people do to keep your neighborhood clean?*

Answer : First and most importantly, don't litter.

People think just a small piece of trash won't make a difference.

The truth is, it does make a big difference.

Secondly, be sure to throw out your garbage every day.

Waste will attract vermin and is very unsanitary.

Finally, make sure your neighbors do the same, because you can't do it alone.

litter〔ˈlɪtɚ〕*v.* 亂丟垃圾　　trash〔træʃ〕*n.* 垃圾
make a difference 有差別；有影響　　***throw out*** 丟出
garbage〔ˈgɑrbɪdʒ〕*n.* 垃圾　　waste〔west〕*n.* 廢棄物
vermin〔ˈvɜmɪn〕*n.* 害蟲（＝*pest*）【老鼠、蚊蠅、跳蚤、蟑螂等】
unsanitary〔ʌnˈsænəˌtɛrɪ〕*adj.* 不衛生的
make sure 確定　　alone〔əˈlon〕*adv.* 獨自

Question 8 : *Do you think learning how to drive will be easy or difficult for you? Please explain.*

Answer : I consider myself a clumsy person.

I've always had a hard time handling mechanical equipment.

So I think learning to drive will be really hard for me.

Even if I learned to drive, I'd probably never go
　　on the road.

The traffic always seems so scary and fast to me.

I guess I'll just stick to the MRT and the bus.

clumsy〔'klʌmzɪ〕*adj.* 笨拙的；笨手笨腳的

have a hard time + V-ing 做～有困難、很辛苦

handle〔'hændl̩〕*v.* 應付

mechanical〔mə'kænɪkl̩〕*adj.* 機械的

equipment〔ɪ'kwɪpmənt〕*n.* 設備；裝備

traffic〔'træfɪk〕*n.*（往來的）車輛；行人

scary〔'skɛrɪ〕*adj.* 可怕的　　***stick to*** 堅持

Answer : I think I'll learn to drive quickly.

I've watched my dad drive ever since I was
　　a kid.

I know all the basics of driving a car.

There are some techniques to driving that my
　　dad taught me.

I think they will help me when I learn to drive.

It should be a piece of cake.

basics〔'besɪks〕*n. pl.* 基礎；原理

technique〔tɛk'nik〕*n.* 技巧

to 可表「歸屬、附加」，作「屬於；歸於」解。例如：the key to
　　the house（房子的鑰匙）。

a piece of cake 容易的事

Question 9 : *If you could choose between living in the mountains or living near a beach, which would you prefer and why? Please explain.*

Answer : I would love to live near a beach.

I love the sun, the sand, and the sea.

It'd make me feel good just looking at the sea.

There might be danger if a storm or typhoon comes.

However, that's a risk I'm willing to take.

To be able to come home to a beach would be a dream come true.

the sun 太陽；陽光   sand〔sænd〕*n.* 沙
take a risk 冒險   willing〔ˈwɪlɪŋ〕*adj.* 願意的
a dream come true 美夢成眞

Answer : I'd prefer to live in the mountains.

Mountains are usually far away from the city.

That would give me a place to relax peacefully.

Living on a mountain would be inconvenient.

Yet the peace that it would bring me would be worth much more.

I'm sure I'd be able to work it out.

peacefully〔ˈpisfəlɪ〕*adv.* 和平地；寧靜地
peace〔pis〕*n.* 平靜；寂靜   worth〔wɝθ〕*adj.* 値得…的
work out 解決（= *solve*）

Question 10 : *Do you have a cell phone? What are some advantages and disadvantages of using a cell phone?*

Answer : I carry my cell phone with me all day.

It makes communication so much easier.

When someone needs me, I'll know immediately.

However, cell phones invade our privacy.

It's really annoying when you're trying to relax
  at home, and the cell phone rings.

That's why I turn it off when I get home.

cell phone 手機
communication〔kə,mjunə'keʃən〕*n.* 溝通；通訊
invade〔ɪn'ved〕*v.* 侵犯   privacy〔'praɪvəsɪ〕*n.* 隱私
annoying〔ə'nɔɪɪŋ〕*adj.* 令人心煩的   *turn off* 關掉

第三部份：看圖敘述

1. This is a picture of a fruit stand.

2. The man in the picture is slicing watermelons and arranging the sliced melons.

3. I like all kinds of fruits, because they are so colorful and tasty.

4. This is an outdoor fruit stand. The man is selling different kinds of melons. He has just cut up a watermelon, and he is arranging the slices on a table. The fruit really looks delicious. The watermelon is juicy. I'm sure he will be able to sell a lot.

【註】 stand〔stænd〕*n.* 攤子
slice〔slaɪs〕*v.* 切薄片　*n.* 一片
watermelon〔'watɚ,mɛlən〕*n.* 西瓜
arrange〔ə'rendʒ〕*v.* 排列
melon〔'mɛlən〕*n.* 甜瓜
colorful〔'kʌləfəl〕*adj.* 顏色鮮豔的；五彩繽紛的
tasty〔'testɪ〕*adj.* 好吃的
cut up 切碎　　juicy〔'dʒusɪ〕*adj.* 多汁的

全民英語能力分級檢定測驗

中級英語檢定複試測驗⑦

寫作能力測驗

本測驗共有兩部份。第一部份為中譯英，第二部份為英文作文。測驗時間為 **40 分鐘**。

一、中譯英（40%）

說明： 請將下列的一段中文翻譯成通順、達意且前後連貫的英文。

　　有一則來自日本的最新報導：有人開辦寵物瑜珈課程，來幫助牠們應付都市生活的壓力。根據研究，長期侷限在狹窄的公寓裡，可能會導致腳掌無力、神經質的吠叫、憂鬱和肥胖。在一次一小時的課程中，寵物被教導瑜珈姿勢，目的在於使牠們放鬆，以保持身心的健康。

二、英文作文（60%）

說明： 請依下面所提供的文字提示寫一篇英文作文，長度約 120 字（8 至 12 個句子）。作文可以是一個完整的段落，也可以分段。（評分重點包括內容、組織、文法、用字遣詞、標點符號、大小寫。）

提示： 在重要考試的前一天，你通常會做些什麼事情？是趕緊再複習一次所有的重點呢？還是放鬆心情、吃個舒服的一餐，再睡個好覺呢？請寫一篇文章描述：準備考試的方法（Preparing for an Exam）。

中級英檢寫作練習

口說能力測驗

請在 15 秒內完成並唸出下列自我介紹的句子：

My seat number is （複試座位號碼後 5 碼）, and my registration number is （初試准考證號碼後 5 碼）.

第一段份：朗讀短文

請先利用一分鐘的時間閱讀下面的短文，然後在二分鐘內以正常的速度，清楚正確的讀出下面的短文，閱讀時請不要發出聲音。

Automobile accidents are as familiar as the common cold but far more deadly. Yet their cause and control remain a serious problem, difficult to solve. Experts have long recognized that this problem has multiple causes; at the very least, it is a "driver-vehicle-roadway" problem. If all drivers exercised good judgment at all times, there would be few accidents. But this is rather like saying that if all people were virtuous, there would be no crime.

*　　　　　*　　　　　*

Honey, you light up my brain! When you're in love, your eyes light up, your face lights up—and apparently, so do four tiny bits of your brain. "It is the common denominator of romantic love," says Bartels, a research fellow at University College London. Bartels examined 11 women and six men who said they were truly in love—statements backed up by psychological tests. When the subjects were shown photographs of their sweethearts, different areas of the brain scan lit up—indicating higher blood flow—than when they were shown pictures of friends. These "love spots" were near, but not the same as, sections that become active when someone is feeling simple lust. Looking at pictures of their dearest also reduced activity in three larger areas of the brain known to be active when people are upset or depressed.

第二部份：回答問題

共十題。題目已事先錄音，每題經由耳機播出二次，不印在試卷上。第一至五題，每題回答時間 15 秒；第六至十題，每題回答時間 30 秒。每題播出後，請立即回答。回答時，不一定要用完整的句子，但請在作答時間內儘量的表達。

第三部份：看圖敘述

下面有一張圖片及四個相關的問題，請在一分半鐘內完成作答。作答時，請直接回答，不需將題號及題目唸出。

首先請利用 30 秒的時間看圖及問題。

1. 這可能是什麼地方？
2. 你認為圖片裡是什麼人呢？
3. 圖片裡的人在做什麼？
4. 請敘述圖片中人物的活動以及景物。

請將下列自我介紹的句子再唸一遍：

My seat number is （複試座位號碼後 5 碼）, and my registration number is （初試准考證號碼後 5 碼）.

口說能力測驗解答

第一部份：朗讀短文

請先利用一分鐘的時間閱讀下面二篇短文，閱讀時請不要發出聲音，
然後在二分鐘之內以正常的速度，清楚正確的讀出下面的短文。

Automobile accidents are as familiar as the common cold but
far more deadly. Yet their cause and control remain a serious
problem, difficult to solve. Experts have long recognized that this
problem has multiple causes; at the very least, it is a "driver-vehicle-
roadway" problem. If all drivers exercised good judgment at all
times, there would be few accidents. But this is rather like saying
that if all people were virtuous, there would be no crime.

【註】 automobile〔ˈɔtəməˌbil〕 *n.* 汽車

common〔ˈkɑmən〕 *adj.* 常見的；普通的　　cold〔kold〕 *n.* 感冒

deadly〔ˈdɛdlɪ〕 *adj.* 致命的　　yet〔jɛt〕 *conj.* 但是

cause〔kɔz〕 *n.* 原因　　remain〔rɪˈmen〕 *v.* 仍然是

solve〔sɑlv〕 *v.* 解決　　expert〔ˈɛkspɜt〕 *n.* 專家

recognize〔ˈrɛkəgˌnaɪz〕 *v.* 認出

multiple〔ˈmʌltəpl̩〕 *adj.* 多樣的　　***at (the very) least*** 至少

vehicle〔ˈviɪkl̩〕 *n.* 車輛　　roadway〔ˈrodˌwe〕 *n.* 道路

exercise〔ˈɛksəˌsaɪz〕 *v.* 運用　　judgment〔ˈdʒʌdʒmənt〕 *n.* 判斷力

at all times 一直　　rather〔ˈræðə〕 *adv.* 有點；相當

virtuous〔ˈvɜtʃʊəs〕 *adj.* 有品德的　　crime〔kraɪm〕 *n.* 罪；犯罪

Honey, you light up my brain! When you're in love, your eyes light up, your face lights up—and apparently, so do four tiny bits of your brain. "It is the common denominator of romantic love," says Bartels, a research fellow at University College London. Bartels examined 11 women and six men who said they were truly in love—statements backed up by psychological tests. When the subjects were shown photographs of their sweethearts, different areas of the brain scan lit up—indicating higher blood flow—than when they were shown pictures of friends. These "love spots" were near, but not the same as, sections that become active when someone is feeling simple lust. Looking at pictures of their dearest also reduced activity in three larger areas of the brain known to be active when people are upset or depressed.

【註】*light up* 點亮；變亮　　apparently〔ə'pɛrəntlɪ〕*adv.* 似乎；看起來
tiny〔'taɪnɪ〕*adj.* 微小的　　bit〔bɪt〕*n.* 一點點；一小塊
denominator〔dɪ'nɑməˌnetə〕*n.* 共同的性質
research〔'risɝtʃ〕*n.* 研究　　fellow〔'fɛlo〕*n.* 人；傢伙；研究人員
examine〔ɪg'zæmɪn〕*v.* 檢查　　statement〔'stetmənt〕*n.* 敘述
back up 支持　　psychological〔ˌsaɪkə'lɑdʒɪkl̩〕*adj.* 心理的
subject〔'sʌbdʒɪkt〕*n.* 受測者　　show〔ʃo〕*v.* 給…看
sweetheart〔'switˌhɑrt〕*n.* 情人；愛人　　scan〔skæn〕*n.* 掃描
indicate〔'ɪndəˌket〕*v.* 顯示　　spot〔spɑt〕*n.* 地點；部位
section〔'sɛkʃən〕*n.* 區域　　active〔'æktɪv〕*adj.* 活躍的
simple〔'sɪmpl̩〕*adj.* 單純的　　lust〔lʌst〕*n.* 肉慾；性慾

dearest〔'dɪrɪst〕*n.* 親愛的；心愛的

activity〔æk'tɪvətɪ〕*n.* 活動；活躍　　upset〔ʌp'sɛt〕*adj.* 不高興的

depressed〔dɪ'prɛst〕*adj.* 沮喪的

第二部份：回答問題

Question 1：*What kind of book do you like to read?*

Answer：I like science fiction.

I love to read about space and the future.

It makes me think that anything is possible.

Some people think it's not good literature.

But I disagree.

There are some great sci-fi novels.

fiction〔'fɪkʃən〕*n.*（虛構的）小說

science fiction 科幻小說　　space〔spes〕*n.* 太空

literature〔'lɪtərətʃə〕*n.* 文學；文學作品

disagree〔͵dɪsə'gri〕*v.* 不同意　　novel〔'nɑvl̩〕*n.* 小說

Answer：I prefer historical novels.

I love being taken back to the past.

I love to feel that I am a part of history.

The books are not only entertaining but educational.

I learn a lot from them.

Reading one is like having an interesting history lesson.

historical〔hɪs'tɔrɪkl̩〕*adj.* 歷史的

entertaining〔͵ɛntə'tenɪŋ〕*adj.* 有趣的

educational〔͵ɛdʒə'keʃənl̩〕*adj.* 教育性的

have a~lesson 上～課

Question 2 : *Did you ever go abroad? Where did you go?*

Answer : Yes, I have been abroad.

I went to Europe with my family.

We went to four countries altogether.

It was a fantastic trip.

We saw medieval castles and beautiful scenery.

I will never forget my time there.

abroad〔ə'brɔd〕*adv.* 到國外　　***go abroad*** 出國

altogether〔͵ɔltə'gɛðɚ〕*adv.* 總共

fantastic〔fæn'tæstɪk〕*adj.* 很棒的

medieval〔͵mɪdɪ'ivl̩〕*adj.* 中世紀的

castle〔'kæsl̩〕*n.* 城堡　　scenery〔'sinərɪ〕*n.* 景色

Answer : No, I've never gone abroad.

I haven't had the time or the money.

But when I finish my education I plan to go.

I want to visit Australia.

I want to dive on the Great Barrier Reef.

I want to see kangaroos and koalas.

visit〔'vɪzɪt〕*v.* 遊覽

Australia〔ɔ'streljə〕*n.* 澳洲　【比較】Austria〔'ɔstrɪə〕*n.* 奧地利

dive〔daɪv〕*v.* 潛水　　barrier〔'bærɪɚ〕*n.* 碉堡；障礙

reef〔rif〕*n.* 礁石　　***the Great Barrier Reef*** 大堡礁

kangaroo〔͵kæŋgə'ru〕*n.* 袋鼠

koala〔ko'ɑlə〕*n.* 無尾熊（= *koala bear* ）

Question 3 ： *What kind of ball game do you like most?*

Answer ： I like basketball.

In fact, I'm crazy about it.

I both watch it and play it.

I began playing when I was in elementary school.

Now I play a game every weekend with my friends.

We're also all big NBA fans.

crazy〔'krezɪ〕*adj.* 瘋狂的；熱中的；狂熱的
be crazy about 很喜歡
elementary〔ˌɛlə'mɛntərɪ〕*adj.* 基本的；初等的
elementary school 小學 (= *primary school*)
NBA 美國籃球聯賽；美國職籃 (= *National Basketball*
　Association)　　fan〔fæn〕*n.* (球、書、影、歌) 迷

Answer ： I love baseball.

I'm glued to the TV during baseball season.

I try never to miss a game.

I also like playing the game even though I'm not
　very good.

My favorite position is second baseman.

I'm working on my catching and throwing skills.

glue〔glu〕*n.* 膠水　*v.* 黏著　　***be glued to*** 黏住；熱中於
season〔'sizn̩〕*n.* (…的) 時期；季節　　***baseball season*** 棒球季
even though 即使　　position〔pə'zɪʃən〕*n.* 位置
baseman〔'besmən〕*n.* 內野手；(一、二、三) 壘手
work on 致力於　　catch〔kætʃ〕*v.* 接住
throw〔θro〕*v.* 投球

Question 4 : *Are you interested in taking a study trip abroad?*

Answer : Yes, of course.

Who wouldn't like to go abroad?

I think I could learn a lot on a study trip.

I'd like to improve my English.

I'd also like to learn more about the culture of Great Britain.

That's why the UK would be my first choice.

study trip 遊學

improve〔ɪmˈpruv〕*v.* 改善

culture〔ˈkʌltʃɚ〕*n.* 文化

Great Britain〔ˈgretˈbrɪtn̩〕*n.* 大不列
顛；英國【英格蘭 England、蘇格蘭
Scotland、威爾斯 Wales 的合稱】

the UK 英國 (= *the United Kingdom*)

Answer : No, I'd rather study here at home.

I think I can concentrate better and learn more.

There would be too many distractions if I went abroad.

I would like to travel overseas someday.

But I want to go as a tourist, not a student.

That way, I can concentrate on having fun!

would rather + *V.* 寧願 < *than* + *V.* >

concentrate〔ˈkɑnsn̩ˌtret〕*v.* 專心 < *on* >

distraction〔dɪˈstrækʃən〕*n.* 令人分心的事物

overseas〔ˈovɚˈsiz〕*adv.* 到國外

someday〔ˈsʌmˌde〕*adv.* 將來有一天

tourist〔ˈtʊrɪst〕*n.* 遊客　　*have fun* 玩得愉快

Question 5：*Have you ever attended a wedding reception? Describe one of your experiences.*

Answer：Yes, I've attended a couple of receptions.

Most recently, I went to my cousin's wedding.

The reception was at a five-star hotel.

The party was great.

There was a lot of really good food.

There was even a live band.

attend〔əˈtɛnd〕*v.* 參加　　wedding〔ˈwɛdɪŋ〕*n.* 婚禮

reception〔rɪˈsɛpʃən〕*n.* 招待會；宴席

a couple of 幾個；兩個　　recently〔ˈrisn̩tlɪ〕*adv.* 最近

cousin〔ˈkʌzn̩〕*n.* 表（堂）兄弟姊妹

live〔laɪv〕*adj.* 現場的　　band〔bænd〕*n.* 樂隊；樂團

Answer：No, I've never been to a wedding.

I'm the oldest of all my cousins.

Everyone says that I'll be the first to marry.

When I do, I'll have a great reception.

I'll follow all of the wedding traditions.

I'll cut the cake with my husband and throw the bouquet.

have been to 曾經去過

marry〔ˈmærɪ〕*v.* 結婚

follow〔ˈfɑlo〕*v.* 遵守

tradition〔trəˈdɪʃən〕*n.* 傳統

bouquet〔buˈke〕*n.* 花束；（新娘的）捧花

Question 6 ： *Describe one of your experiences with a teacher.*

Answer ： I still remember my first grade teacher.

She was very kind to me.

She also taught me about confidence.

When I began school, it was difficult for me to read.

She told me to believe in myself.

I did, and I succeeded.

grade〔gred〕*n.* 年級
confidence〔'kɑnfədəns〕*n.* 信心；自信
begin school 開始上學
believe in 對～有信心；相信～的存在；相信～是好的、是對的

Answer ： I liked most of my teachers in school.

But there was one I could not get along with.

She always blamed us without listening to us.

Sometimes she explained things too quickly, and

　I couldn't understand.

She said that was my own fault.

She blamed me for not paying attention.

get along with *sb.* 與某人相處
blame〔blem〕*v.* 責怪 *<for sth.>*
explain〔ɪk'splen〕*v.* 說明；解釋
fault〔fɔlt〕*n.* 過錯　　***pay attention*** 注意

Question 7 : *Your friend flunked an exam and felt very frustrated.*
Say something to cheer him or her up.

Answer : I heard about your exam.

Don't feel too bad.

Everyone fails sometimes.

You can do better next time.

Think of this as an opportunity.

Learn from your mistakes.

flunk〔flʌŋk〕*v.*（考試）不及格（= *fail*）
frustrated〔'frʌstretɪd〕*adj.* 受挫的
cheer** sb*. ***up 使某人振作精神
do better 考得好；表現得更好　【比較】*do well* 考得好
think of A as B 認為 A 是 B（= *regard A as B*）
opportunity〔,ɑpə'tjunətɪ〕*n.* 機會

Question 8 : *How to be a popular person?*

Answer : Being popular is easy.

All you have to do is treat others well.

Be kind and considerate.

Also, show that you're interested.

Ask people about themselves.

Everyone likes to talk to a friend.

***All** one **has to do is V**.* 某人所必須做的就是…
treat〔trit〕*v.* 對待
considerate〔kən'sɪdərɪt〕*adj.* 體貼的（= *thoughtful*）
show〔ʃo〕*v.* 表現；顯示

Question 9 : *Pearl milk tea is one of the most popular drinks in Taiwan. What do you think of it?*

Answer : I love pearl milk tea.

It's one of my favorite drinks.

I love the sweet taste.

It's also unique.

It started in Taiwan, and it has spread around the world.

It's something we can be proud of.

pearl〔pɝl〕*n.* 珍珠　　***pearl milk tea*** 珍珠奶茶
taste〔test〕*n.* 味道
unique〔ju'nik〕*adj.* 獨特的；獨一無二的
spread〔sprɛd〕*v.* 散播　　***be proud of*** 以～為榮

Answer : I don't really care for it.

I find it too sweet.

I also don't like the pearls.

They're tasteless in my opinion.

And they always get stuck in the straw.

It's just not worth it.

care for 喜歡【用於否定句和疑問句】
find〔faɪnd〕*v.* 覺得　　tasteless〔'testlɪs〕*adj.* 沒味道的
in* one's *opinion 依某人之見　　stick〔stɪk〕*v.* 使卡住
straw〔strɔ〕*n.* 吸管；稻草　　worth〔wɝθ〕*adj.* 值得…的
worth it 值得的（=*worthwhile*）

Question 10 ： *Introduce one of your favorite dishes and how to make it.*

Answer ： One of my favorite dishes is fried rice.

I like it because it's tasty and also easy to make.

All you need is cooked rice and a few other ingredients.

I fry the rice together with onions, garlic and
　　some vegetables.

Sometimes I add meat or eggs or seafood.

It's different every time I make it.

dish〔dɪʃ〕*n.* 菜餚
fried rice 炒飯【炒麵則為 fried noodles 或 chow mien】
tasty〔'testɪ〕*adj.* 好吃的；美味的
ingredient〔ɪn'gridɪənt〕*n.* 材料　　fry〔fraɪ〕*v.* 炒
together with 連同　　onion〔'ʌnjən〕*n.* 洋蔥
garlic〔'gɑrlɪk〕*n.* 大蒜　　add〔æd〕*v.* 加
meat〔mit〕*n.* 肉　　seafood〔'si,fud〕*n.* 海鮮

Answer ： My favorite dish is fried chicken.

I've never made it, though.

I usually buy it when I go out to eat.

But I think it's not too hard to make.

All you need is some chicken, some batter, and some hot oil.

Maybe I'll try it sometime!

though〔ðo〕*adv.* 不過【置於句中或句尾】
fried chicken 炸雞【fry 可指「煎」、「炒」或「炸」】
batter〔'bætɚ〕*n.* 麵衣；蛋、麵粉、水或牛奶和成的糊狀物
　　（= *mixture of flour, milk and egg*）【用以調製薄煎餅或油炸食物】
sometime〔'sʌm,taɪm〕*adv.* 某時

第三部份：看圖敘述

1. This is a classroom. I believe it is a university classroom because the students are not wearing uniforms.

2. The people in the picture are students, who are mostly male, and one teacher, who is a woman.

3. The woman is giving a lecture and the students are listening to her.

4. This is a large, bright classroom with big windows. There is a chalkboard at the front of the room, which is partially obscured by a screen. The teacher is using PowerPoint in her lesson and there is a weather map projected on the screen. The students look interested in what she is saying.

【註】 uniform (ˈjunəˌfɔrm) n. 制服　　mostly (ˈmostlɪ) adv. 大多
lecture (ˈlɛktʃə) n. 講課　　***give a lecture*** 講課
chalkboard (ˈtʃɔkˌbord) n. (淡色的) 黑板　　front (frʌnt) n. 前面
partially (ˈpɑrʃəlɪ) adv. 部分地　　obscure (əbˈskjur) v. 遮蔽
screen (skrin) n. 螢幕　　project (prəˈdʒɛkt) v. 投射；投影

全民英語能力分級檢定測驗

中級英語檢定複試測驗⑧

寫作能力測驗

本測驗共有兩部份。第一部份爲中譯英,第二部份爲英文作文。測驗時間爲 **40分鐘**。

一、中譯英（40 %）

說明： 請將下列的一段中文翻譯成通順、達意且前後連貫的英文。

　　我心情不好的時候,常常邀朋友去打籃球。打籃球時,我必須專心把球投進籃框。這麼一來,我就可以暫時忘記煩惱。打完球後,我會和朋友談談令我困擾的事情。通常,我會接受他們寶貴的建議,努力使自己再快樂起來。

二、英文作文（60 %）

說明： 請依下面所提供的文字提示寫一篇英文作文,長度約120字（8至12個句子）。作文可以是一個完整的段落,也可以分段。（評分重點包括內容、組織、文法、用字遣詞、標點符號、大小寫。）

提示： 你曾經到醫院探視過親友嗎？請描述一次探病的經驗（A Hospital Visit）,說明：你探視誰、他爲何住院、你帶了什麼東西給他、對他說了什麼話等等。

中級英檢寫作練習

口說能力測驗

請在15秒內完成並唸出下列自我介紹的句子：

My seat number is （複試座位號碼後5碼）, and my registration number is （初試准考證號碼後5碼）.

第一段份：朗讀短文

請先利用一分鐘的時間閱讀下面的短文，然後在二分鐘內以正常的速度，清楚正確的讀出下面的短文，閱讀時請不要發出聲音。

The cold weather is expected to continue today, with only a slight rise in the temperature before the weather warms up more noticeably on Wednesday, local media reported, citing Central Weather Bureau officials. The rain is also expected to continue until Wednesday, with sea travelers warned to watch out for heavy mists, bureau officials said. Due to a cold front circling the island, yesterday was one of the coldest days this year. In Tamshui near Taipei, the temperatures hit a low of 5.3 degrees Celsius, the second coldest day for the harbor city this year. Temperatures in Taipei also reached similar lows of 7.2 degrees.

*　　　　　　*　　　　　　*

As if winning 11 Oscars was not enough, fantasy epic "Lord of the Rings" is ambitiously trying to become even more popular by becoming a lavish stage musical, a British newspaper said Sunday. Producers are planning to turn the last of three film installments, which swept the board at the Academy Awards, into the most expensive musical ever seen in London, the Sunday Telegraph said. The eight million pound (12 million euro, US$14 million) production will see dozens of actors portray hobbits, elves, wizards and orcs in complex battle scenes, the report said.

第二部份：回答問題

共十題。題目已事先錄音，每題經由耳機播出二次，不印在試卷上。第一至五題，每題回答時間 15 秒；第六至十題，每題回答時間 30 秒。每題播出後，請立即回答。回答時，不一定要用完整的句子，但請在作答時間內儘量的表達。

第三部份：看圖敘述

下面有一張圖片及四個相關的問題，請在一分半鐘內完成作答。作答時，請直接回答，不需將題號及題目唸出。

首先請利用 30 秒的時間看圖及問題。

1. 這可能是什麼地方？
2. 圖片裡的人在做什麼？
3. 你和圖片裡的人有過相同經驗嗎？
4. 請敘述圖片中人物的活動以及景物。

請將下列自我介紹的句子再唸一遍：

My seat number is（複試座位號碼後 5 碼）, and my registration number is（初試准考證號碼後 5 碼）.

口說能力測驗解答

第一部份：朗讀短文

請先利用一分鐘的時間閱讀下面二篇短文，閱讀時請不要發出聲音，然後在二分鐘之內以正常的速度，清楚正確的讀出下面的短文。

The cold weather is expected to continue today, with only a slight rise in the temperature before the weather warms up more noticeably on Wednesday, local media reported, citing Central Weather Bureau officials. The rain is also expected to continue until Wednesday, with sea travelers warned to watch out for heavy mists, bureau officials said. Due to a cold front circling the island, yesterday was one of the coldest days this year. In Tamshui near Taipei, the temperatures hit a low of 5.3 degrees Celsius, the second coldest day for the harbor city this year. Temperatures in Taipei also reached similar lows of 7.2 degrees.

【註】 slight〔slaɪt〕adj. 稍微的　　rise〔raɪz〕n. 上升
warm up 變溫暖　　noticeably〔'notɪsəblɪ〕adv. 明顯地
local〔'lokḷ〕adj. 當地的　　media〔'midɪə〕n. pl. 媒體
cite〔saɪt〕v. 引用　　bureau〔'bjʊro〕n. 局；處
official〔ə'fɪʃəl〕n. 官員；職員　　***sea traveler*** 航海人（= *voyager*）
watch out for 小心　　heavy〔'hɛvɪ〕adj. 濃密的
mist〔mɪst〕n. 霧　　***due to*** 由於　　front〔frʌnt〕n.【氣象】鋒面
cold front 冷鋒　　circle〔'sɝkḷ〕v. 包圍；籠罩
hit〔hɪt〕v. 達到　　low〔lo〕n. 最低紀錄；最低數字
degree〔dɪ'grɪ〕n. 度　　Celsius〔'sɛlsɪəs〕adj. 攝氏的
harbor〔'hɑrbɚ〕n. 港口　　similar〔'sɪmələ〕adj. 相似的

As if winning 11 Oscars was not enough, fantasy epic "Lord of the Rings" is ambitiously trying to become even more popular by becoming a lavish stage musical, a British newspaper said Sunday. Producers are planning to turn the last of three film installments, which swept the board at the Academy Awards, into the most expensive musical ever seen in London, the Sunday Telegraph said. The eight million pound (12 million euro, US$14 million) production will see dozens of actors portray hobbits, elves, wizards and orcs in complex battle scenes, the report said.

【註】 ***as if*** 就好像　　Oscar〔'ɔskɚ〕*n.* 奧斯卡獎
fantasy〔'fæntəsɪ〕*n.* 幻想；想像
epic〔'ɛpɪk〕*n.* 史詩；敘事詩
Lord of the Rings 魔戒
ambitiously〔æm'bɪʃəslɪ〕*adv.* 野心勃勃地
lavish〔'lævɪʃ〕*adj.* 奢華的
stage〔stedʒ〕*n.* 舞台
musical〔'mjuzʊkḷ〕*n.* 音樂劇　　***turn*** A ***into*** B 把 A 變成 B
installment〔ɪn'stɔlmənt〕*n.* 一回；一册
sweep the board 贏得所有獎項　　academy〔ə'kædəmɪ〕*n.* 學院
award〔ə'wɔrd〕*n.* 獎　　***Academy Award*** 奧斯卡金像獎
telegraph〔'tɛlə,græf〕*n.* 電報　　pound〔paʊnd〕*n.* 英鎊
euro〔'juro〕*n.* 歐元　　production〔prə'dʌkʃən〕*n.* 上演的作品
see〔si〕*v.* 使（某人）做…　　***dozens of*** 數十個
portray〔por'tre〕*v.* 飾演　　hobbit〔'hɑbɪt〕*n.* 哈比人
elf〔ɛlf〕*n.* 小精靈　　wizard〔'wɪzɚd〕*n.* 巫師
orc〔ɔrk〕*n.* 妖魔　　complex〔kəm'plɛks〕*adj.* 複雜的
battle〔'bætḷ〕*n.* 戰爭　　scene〔sin〕*n.* 場景

第二部份：回答問題

Question 1： *Do you have any experience of working part time?*

Answer： Yes, I had a part-time job last summer.

I worked in a convenience store near my house.

I liked the job, but it was a little boring at times.

The best thing about it was my co-workers.

It was fun being part of a team.

And, of course, I also liked having some spending money!

part time 兼職地【「全職地」則是 full time】
part-time *adj.* 兼職的　*convenience store* 便利商店
a little 有一點　*at times* 有時候（= *sometimes*）
co-worker〔'ko,wɜkɚ〕*n.* 同事　fun〔fʌn〕*adj.* 有趣的
team〔tim〕*n.* 團隊　*spending money* 零用錢

Answer： No, I've never worked part time.

When I'm not studying, I just relax with my hobbies.

I also hang out with my friends.

I think it's important for me to concentrate on school now.

Relaxing is also important because it relieves stress.

I'll have the chance to work after I graduate.

hobby〔'hɑbɪ〕*n.* 嗜好
hang out 閒混；和～在一起 <*with*>
school〔skul〕*n.* 學業　relieve〔rɪ'liv〕*v.* 減輕
stress〔strɛs〕*n.* 壓力　graduate〔'grædʒʊ,et〕*v.* 畢業

Question 2： *Do you like taking pictures? Why or why not?*

Answer： Yes, I love taking pictures.

It's a great way to preserve memories.

I can look at the photos later and remember the
good times.

Photography can also be a kind of art.
I like taking pictures of landscapes as well as people.
Someday I will frame the best ones and hang them
on the wall.

take a picture 拍照　　preserve〔prɪ'zɝv〕v. 保存
memory〔'mɛmərɪ〕n. 記憶；回憶
photo〔'foto〕n. 照片（= *photograph*）
photography〔fə'tɑgrəfɪ〕n. 攝影
landscape〔'læn(d)ˌskep〕n. 風景
as well as 以及　　frame〔frem〕v. 給…裝框

Answer：No, I rarely take pictures.
I don't like to carry a camera around with me.
I'd rather just enjoy the moment.

Besides, I'm not a very good photographer.
My pictures never turn out well.
I'd rather just buy a postcard.

rarely〔'rɛrlɪ〕adv. 很少　　carry〔'kærɪ〕v. 攜帶
around〔ə'raʊnd〕adv. 到處　　*would rather* 寧願
turn out ~ 結果是~；結局是~
postcard〔'postˌkɑrd〕n. 明信片

Question 3：*Do you like growing up? Why or why not?*

Answer：I'm excited about growing up.
I like trying new things and facing new challenges.
I look forward to the day I will be an adult.

I'll have more responsibility then.

But I'm sure that I'll be able to handle it.

I'll make my own decisions and face the consequences.

grow up 長大　　face〔fes〕*v.* 面對
challenge〔'tʃælɪndʒ〕*n.* 挑戰
look forward to + *N./V-ing* 期待　　adult〔ə'dʌlt〕*n.* 成人
responsibility〔rɪ,spɑnsə'bɪlətɪ〕*n.* 責任
handle〔'hændl〕*v.* 處理；應付　　decision〔dɪ'sɪʒən〕*n.* 決定
consequence〔'kɑnsə,kwɛns〕*n.* 後果

Answer : I have mixed feelings about growing up.

Being a kid has been great.

All I have to do is learn.

My parents take good care of me.

I don't have to worry about anything.

I'll be sorry to leave childhood behind.

mixed〔mɪkst〕*adj.* 混合的；互相矛盾的
all one ***has to do is*** *V*. 某人所必須要做的就是…
leave ~ ***behind*** 留下~；遺忘~

Question 4 : *How do you go to school or work every day? What do you do during the commute?*

Answer : It takes me about half an hour to get to school.

I take a bus from a stop near my home.

It's usually not crowded, so I can sit down during the trip.

On the way to school I usually read over my notes.

I also listen to music on my mp3 player.

It makes the time fly.

commute〔kə'mjut〕*n.* 通勤　　stop〔stɑp〕*n.* 停車站
crowded〔'kraʊdɪd〕*adj.* 擁擠的　　trip〔trɪp〕*n.* 行程

on the way to 在~的途中　　read over 讀完
notes〔nots〕*n. pl.* 筆記　　fly〔flaɪ〕*v.* (時間) 飛逝

Question 5 ： *Have you ever checked books out from the library?*
Describe your experience.

Answer ： Yes, I often take books out of the local library.
They have a good collection of novels and DVDs.
I like to do this during the holidays.

To check out the books, I have to show my library card.
Then I can keep them for up to two weeks.
I always return them on time.

check out (從圖書館) 借出
collection〔kəˈlɛkʃən〕*n.* 收集；收藏
have a good collection of 收藏很多
library card 借書證　　*up to* 多達；高達
return〔rɪˈtɜn〕*v.* 歸還　　*on time* 準時

Question 6 ： *Do you have any experience of running into an old*
friend you haven't seen for a long time?

Answer ： Yes.　Once I ran into a friend from elementary school.
We hadn't seen each other in about three years.
It was quite a surprise.

We decided to catch up, so we went to a coffee shop.
Then we exchanged phone numbers and email addresses.
We still communicate with each other now and then.

run into 偶然遇到　　*quite a* 不尋常的；非凡的
catch up 追趕上 (落後的進度)；敘舊
exchange〔ɪksˈtʃendʒ〕*v.* 交換
email〔ˈiˌmel〕*n.* 電子郵件 (= e-mail)

communicate〔kən'mjunəˌket〕*v.* 溝通；聯絡
now and then 偶爾；有時候

Question 7 : ***Can you ride a bicycle?***

Answer : Yes, I can.
I learned to ride a bike when I was about six years old.
My father taught me how to ride.

Now I often ride my bike around town.
I don't ride it to school, but I use it when go to my
　friends' houses.
I also ride it around the park for exercise.

Question 8 : ***Do you speak Taiwanese? How is your Taiwanese?***

Answer : Yes, I can speak Taiwanese.
My grandparents often speak it with me.
I grew up listening to it.

My comprehension is pretty good.
But sometimes it's hard to express myself.
Still, it's nice to know my grandparents' language.

Taiwanese〔ˌtaɪwɑ'niz〕*n.* 台語
comprehension〔ˌkɑmprɪ'hɛnʃən〕*n.* 理解
pretty〔'prɪtɪ〕*adv.* 相當地　　express〔ɪk'sprɛs〕*v.* 表達
express *oneself* 表達自己的意思

Answer : No, I don't really speak Taiwanese.
I can understand a little bit.
I often hear it in the markets.

But I don't like to speak it.

I think my accent sounds funny.

I'm afraid people will laugh at me.

a little bit 一點點   market〔'mɑrkɪt〕*n.* 市場
accent〔'æksɛnt〕*n.* 口音；腔調
funny〔'fʌnɪ〕*adj.* 好笑的   *laugh at* 嘲笑

Question 9 : *What kind of fruit do you like? Give some examples.*

Answer : I like tropical fruits.

Luckily we have quite a few in Taiwan.

We also import many from Southeast Asia.

Pineapple, mango, and starfruit are among my favorites.

I love the sweet and sour flavor.

I wish I could eat them all year round.

tropical〔'trɑpɪkl̩〕*adj.* 熱帶的
luckily〔'lʌkɪlɪ〕*adv.* 幸運地；幸運的是
quite a few 很多（= *many*）   import〔ɪm'port〕*v.* 進口
Southeast Asia 東南亞   pineapple〔'paɪnˌæpl̩〕*n.* 鳳梨
mango〔'mæŋgo〕*n.* 芒果   starfruit〔'stɑrˌfrut〕*n.* 楊桃
favorite〔'fevərɪt〕*n.* 最喜愛的事物或人
sour〔saʊr〕*adj.* 酸的   flavor〔'flevɚ〕*n.* 味道；口味
all (the) year round 一整年；一年到頭

Answer : My favorite fruit is the strawberry.

I love the flavor, and it's good for me too.

It's really high in vitamin C.

I always eat a lot of strawberries when they are in season.

I only wish the season were longer.

I wish I could eat them all the time.

strawberry〔'strɔˌbɛrɪ〕*n.* 草莓   *be high in* 富含

vitamin〔'vaɪtəmɪn〕*n.* 維他命；維生素
in season 在盛產期、當季、旺季（↔ *out of season*）
all the time 一直；總是

Question 10 : *Is your room always a mess or do you always keep it tidy?*

Answer : My room is usually neat.

I clean it every weekend in order to keep it that way.

Otherwise, I think it would be a mess.

I enjoy having a tidy room.

It helps me to stay organized.

I can find everything I need quickly.

mess〔mɛs〕*n.* 亂七八糟；凌亂
tidy〔'taɪdɪ〕*adj.* 整齊的；整潔的　neat〔nit〕*adj.* 整齊的
***in order to* V**. 以便於～　otherwise〔'ʌðɚ,waɪz〕*adv.* 否則
organized〔'ɔrgən,aɪzd〕*adj.* 有組織的；有條理的

Answer : Unfortunately, my room is rather messy.

I rarely put my things where they belong.

There are often clothes and papers scattered about.

My mother complains about this, of course.

I always say I'll clean it up, but I never do.

I guess I've learned to live with it.

unfortunately〔ʌn'fɔrtʃənɪtlɪ〕*adv.* 不幸地；遺憾地
rather〔'ræðɚ〕*adv.* 相當地　messy〔'mɛsɪ〕*adj.* 雜亂的
belong〔bə'lɔŋ〕*v.* 屬於；該在～地方
scatter〔'skætɚ〕*v.* 散播；散置；亂丟
about〔ə'baʊt〕*adv.* 到處～　complain〔kəm'plen〕*v.* 抱怨
clean up 把…打掃乾淨　***live with*** 忍耐；忍受

第三部份：看圖敘述

1. This is an MRT station.

2. Some of the people are standing in line, waiting to board the train. Others are exiting the car.

3. Yes, I have ridden the MRT several times, but sometimes the crowd is not so orderly!

4. The MRT train is standing in the station. The doors of the car are open and a man and a woman in jackets are exiting the car. There is a short line of people waiting to get on. It must be winter because everyone is wearing heavy clothes. One woman in the background is taking a picture.

【註】 ***stand in line*** 排隊　　board〔bord〕*v.* 上（車）（= *get on*）
train〔tren〕*n.* 列車　　exit〔ˈɛksɪt, ˈɛgzɪt〕*v.* 離開
car〔kɑr〕*n.* 車廂　　crowd〔krɑʊd〕*n.* 群眾
orderly〔ˈɔrdɚlɪ〕*adj.* 有秩序的　　stand〔stænd〕*v.* 停著
line〔laɪn〕*n.* 一排；行列　　background〔ˈbækˌgrɑʊnd〕*n.* 背景

全民英語能力分級檢定測驗
中級英語檢定複試測驗⑨

寫作能力測驗

本測驗共有兩部份。第一部份為中譯英,第二部份為英文作文。測驗時間為 **40 分鐘**。

一、中譯英(40％)

說明: 請將下列的一段中文翻譯成通順、達意且前後連貫的英文。

我們和別人說話時必須謹慎。說話不經考慮,容易導致不希望看到的結果,例如:溝通不良、傷害,或更糟的是,爭吵。友誼破裂常常也是因為如此。除了慎選我們說的話之外,說話前更應仔細考慮。話一旦說出口,造成的傷害有時候就無法彌補了。

二、英文作文(60％)

說明: 請依下面所提供的文字提示寫一篇英文作文,長度約 120 字(8 至 12 個句子)。作文可以是一個完整的段落,也可以分段。(評分重點包括內容、組織、文法、用字遣詞、標點符號、大小寫。)

提示: 未來某一天,你或許會有家庭和小孩。身為父母,責任重大,你會如何養育國家的幼苗呢?會有什麼要求呢?請寫一篇文章說明:
如果你為人父母(If I Were a Parent),你會如何養育小孩呢?

中級英檢寫作練習

口說能力測驗

請在 15 秒內完成並唸出下列自我介紹的句子：

My seat number is （複試座位號碼後 5 碼）, and my registration number is （初試准考證號碼後 5 碼）.

第一段份：朗讀短文

Millions of Americans eat turkey only once or twice a year. The first time is on the fourth Thursday of November, which is Thanksgiving Day. A large roasted turkey is the centerpiece of the Thanksgiving meal in the United States. Because turkey is the most common main dish for a Thanksgiving dinner, Thanksgiving is sometimes colloquially called Turkey Day. The second time is on Christmas, December 25. Housewives rarely buy turkeys except for one of these holiday dinners. Why? Because the birds are big and take many hours to cook.

*　　　　　　*　　　　　　*

The buzzing electric toothbrush of a former wife of James Bond star Sean Connery sparked a security alert at an Australian airport on Sunday. Diane Cilento, who was once married to Connery, told national news agency Australian Associated Press that she was on a Virgin Blue plane due to leave the eastern city of Brisbane for the northern city of Cairns around midday Sunday when she was asked to return to the terminal. "I was called off the plane and they had my bag there and they knew my name and they wouldn't go near it because there was a terrible noise coming from it," she said. "They made me open it, and it was my toothbrush."

第二部份：回答問題

共十題。題目已事先錄音，每題經由耳機播出二次，不印在試卷上。第一至五題，每題回答時間 15 秒；第六至十題，每題回答時間 30 秒。每題播出後，請立即回答。回答時，不一定要用完整的句子，但請在作答時間內儘量的表達。

第三部份：看圖敘述

下面有一張圖片及四個相關的問題，請在一分半鐘內完成作答。作答時，請直接回答，不需將題號及題目唸出。

首先請利用 30 秒的時間看圖及問題。

1. 這可能是什麼地方？
2. 照片裡的人在做什麼？
3. 你來過這樣的地方嗎？你喜歡嗎？
4. 請敘述圖片中人物的活動以及景物。

請將下列自我介紹的句子再唸一遍：

My seat number is （複試座位號碼後 5 碼）, and my registration number is （初試准考證號碼後 5 碼）.

口說能力測驗解答

第一部份：朗讀短文

請先利用一分鐘的時間閱讀下面二篇短文，閱讀時請不要發出聲音，然後在二分鐘之內以正常的速度，清楚正確的讀出下面的短文。

Millions of Americans eat turkey only once or twice a year. The first time is on the fourth Thursday of November, which is Thanksgiving Day. A large roasted turkey is the centerpiece of the Thanksgiving meal in the United States. Because turkey is the most common main dish for a Thanksgiving dinner, Thanksgiving is sometimes colloquially called Turkey Day. The second time is on Christmas, December 25. Housewives rarely buy turkeys except for one of these holiday dinners. Why? Because the birds are big and take many hours to cook.

【註】 turkey〔ˈtɝkɪ〕 n. 火雞
Thanksgiving〔ˌθæŋksˈgɪvɪŋ〕 n. 感恩節（ = *Thanksgiving Day* ）
roast〔rost〕 v.（用烤箱）烤
centerpiece〔ˈsɛntɚˌpis〕 n. 最重要的部分；核心
（ = *focus* = *core* = *heart* ）　　meal〔mil〕 n. 一餐
dish〔dɪʃ〕 n.（一道）菜　　dinner〔ˈdɪnɚ〕 n. 大餐
colloquially〔kəˈlokwɪəlɪ〕 adv. 口語地
housewife〔ˈhausˌwaɪf〕 n. 家庭主婦
rarely〔ˈrɛrlɪ〕 adv. 很少
except for 除了～之外

The buzzing electric toothbrush of a former wife of James Bond star Sean Connery sparked a security alert at an Australian airport on Sunday. Diane Cilento, who was once married to Connery, told national news agency Australian Associated Press that she was on a Virgin Blue plane due to leave the eastern city of Brisbane for the northern city of Cairns around midday Sunday when she was asked to return to the terminal. "I was called off the plane and they had my bag there and they knew my name and they wouldn't go near it because there was a terrible noise coming from it," she said. "They made me open it, and it was my toothbrush."

【註】 buzz〔bʌz〕v. 發出嗡嗡聲
electric〔ɪ'lɛktrɪk〕adj. 電動的
toothbrush〔'tuθ,brʌʃ〕n. 牙刷
former〔'fɔrmɚ〕adj. 前任的
James Bond 詹姆士・龐德【007電影的男主角】
Sean Connery〔'ʃɔn 'kɑnərɪ〕n. 史恩・康納萊
spark〔spɑrk〕v. 引起   security〔sɪ'kjʊrətɪ〕n. 安全
alert〔ə'lɝt〕n. 警報；警戒
Diane Cilento〔daɪ'ɛn sɪ'lɛnto〕n. 黛安・奇倫托
be married to 和…結婚   **news agency** 通訊社
associated〔ə'soʃɪ,etɪd〕adj. 聯合的
press〔prɛs〕n. 印刷；新聞界   **Virgin Blue** 維珍航空公司
due〔dju〕adj. 預定的
Brisbane〔'brɪzbən〕n. 布里斯班【澳洲東部都市，昆士蘭首府】
Cairns〔kɛrnz〕n. 凱恩斯【位於昆士蘭省，大堡礁所在地】
midday〔'mɪd,de〕n. 正午；中午
terminal〔'tɝmənḷ〕n.（機場）航空站   off〔ɔf〕prep. 從…下來

第二部份：回答問題

Question 1 ： *Introduce one or two websites you frequently use*.

Answer ： I often go to the Wikipedia website.

It's an online encyclopedia.

It helps me find the answers to questions fast.

I know the entries aren't 100 percent accurate.

But it's good for general information.

I love it because it's convenient.

website（'wɛb,saɪt）*n.* 網站
frequently（'frikwəntlɪ）*adv.* 經常
online（'ɑn,laɪn）*adj.* 線上的
encyclopedia（ɪn,saɪklə'pidɪə）*n.* 百科全書
entry（'ɛntrɪ）*n.*（字典中的）字；項目；條目
accurate（'ækjərɪt）*adj.* 正確的
general（'dʒɛnərəl）*adj.* 一般的

Answer ： I often go to a site called English Club.

It's a website for English language learners.

There's a lot of helpful information on it.

I had to register and become a member.

But the service is free.

It's a fun and easy way to improve my English.

register（'rɛdʒɪstɚ）*v.* 登記；註冊　　member（'mɛmbɚ）*n.* 會員
free（fri）*adj.* 免費的　　fun（fʌn）*adj.* 有趣的
improve（ɪm'pruv）*v.* 改善；使進步

Question 2 ： *What do you think of people talking loudly in public places?*

Answer ： It really bothers me when people talk loudly.

I think it's impolite.

It shows that they don't care about others.

They are thinking only of their conversation.

They aren't paying attention to their surroundings.

They really disturb the peace!

public place 公共場所　　bother〔'bɑðɚ〕*v.* 困擾
impolite〔͵ɪmpə'laɪt〕*adj.* 不禮貌的　　*care about* 在意
think of 想到　　*pay attention to* 注意
surroundings〔sə'raʊndɪŋz〕*n. pl.* 周圍環境
disturb〔dɪ'stɝb〕*v.* 打擾；擾亂　　peace〔pis〕*n.* 寧靜

Question 3 ： *What time do you usually go to bed now?*

Answer ： These days I'm trying to go to bed early.

I think that keeping early hours is good for me.

Getting enough sleep helps me to concentrate in school.

So I usually turn in by ten o'clock.

I eat dinner around seven.

Then I read or watch TV until ten.

these days 最近　　*keep early hours* 早睡早起
concentrate〔'kɑnsn͵tret〕*v.* 專心　　*turn in* 睡覺
by〔baɪ〕*prep.* 在…之前

Question 4 : *Are you an efficient person?*

Answer : Yes, I think I'm efficient.

I can get my work done fairly quickly.

I never hand anything in late.

I also don't waste time.

When I sit down to do something, I just work at it

until I'm done.

I'm not easily distracted.

efficient〔ə'fɪʃənt〕*adj.* 有效率的
fairly〔'fɛrlɪ〕*adv.* 相當地
hand in 繳交　　*work at* 研究；從事
distract〔dɪ'strækt〕*v.* 使分心

Answer : I wish I were efficient, but I'm not.

It often takes me a long time to do things.

I think it's because I try to do too much at a time.

I should concentrate on just one task at a time.

That way I'll avoid wasting time.

It will make my life a lot easier.

at a time 一次　　*concentrate on* 專心於
task〔tæsk〕*n.* 任務；工作　　*that way* 那樣的話
avoid〔ə'vɔɪd〕*v.* 避免　　easy〔'izɪ〕*adj.* 輕鬆的

Question 5 ：*Describe one of your family get-togethers. What was the occasion, who went and what did you do?*

Answer ：My family got together just last week.

It was my father's birthday.

All of my aunts, uncles, and cousins came.

We had a big dinner together.

Mom cooked all of Dad's favorite dishes.

We ate and talked for hours.

get-together〔'gɛttə,gɛðɚ〕*n.* 聚會

occasion〔ə'keʒən〕*n.* 場合　　***get together*** 聚會；團聚

cousin〔'kʌzn̩〕*n.* 表（堂）兄弟姊妹　　have〔hæv〕*v.* 吃

big〔bɪg〕*adj.* 豐盛的　　dish〔dɪʃ〕*n.* 菜餚

Answer ：My family always gets together at New Year, of course.

We always gather at my grandparents' home.

They live in a small village in central Taiwan.

Last year, all of my relatives were there as usual.

We ate a lot of good food.

We also played card games.

gather〔'gæðɚ〕*v.* 聚集　　village〔'vɪlɪdʒ〕*n.* 村莊

central〔'sɛntrəl〕*adj.* 中央的　　relative〔'rɛlətɪv〕*n.* 親戚

as usual 像往常一樣　　***card game*** 撲克牌遊戲

Question 6 ： ***What did you do during the past New Year holiday?***

Answer ： Last New Year holiday was very special for me.

My family traveled abroad for the first time.

We went to Japan for one week.

It was a great experience for all of us.

We tried new foods and saw wonderful scenery.

We even saw snow!

abroad〔ə'brɔd〕*adv.* 到國外

for the first time 第一次

scenery〔'sinərɪ〕*n.* 風景

Answer ： Last year I went to my grandparents' home.

This is what I do every year.

They live in Taipei, so I didn't have to travel too far.

My grandmother cooked a delicious meal.

My uncles and aunts gave me red envelopes.

I played a lot of games with my cousins.

travel〔'trævl̩〕*v.* 旅行；行進；前進

meal〔mil〕*n.* 一餐

red envelope 紅包

Question 7 : *Have you ever had Japanese food? How do you like it?*

Answer : Yes, I've eaten Japanese food.

I like it very much.

There is a good Japanese restaurant that I go to with
  my parents.

I like Japanese food because it tastes very fresh.

I love sushi and sashimi.

It's a special experience to eat it.

fresh〔frɛʃ〕*adj.* 新鮮的

sushi〔'suʃɪ〕*n.* 壽司

sashimi〔sɑ'ʃimi〕*n.* 生魚片

Answer : I've tried Japanese food, but I don't like it very much.

I'm not that fond of seafood, and I definitely don't
  like sushi.

I just can't eat raw fish!

The other dishes are OK, but not very filling.

I always feel hungry after a Japanese meal.

I prefer more traditional food, I guess.

be fond of 喜歡   seafood〔'si,fud〕*n.* 海鮮

definitely〔'dɛfənɪtlɪ〕*adv.* 絕對（不）【用於否定句】

raw〔rɔ〕*adj.* 生的   filling〔'fɪlɪŋ〕*adj.* 填飽肚子的

traditional〔trə'dɪʃənḷ〕*adj.* 傳統的

Question 8 : *Have you ever solved a difficult problem on your own?*
Please describe your experience.

Answer : Yes. I once got lost in a big city.

I had to find my way by myself.

I didn't speak the language, so I couldn't ask anyone.

I solved the problem by using my map.

I looked at the street signs until I figured out where I was.

Then I plotted a route back to my hotel.

solve〔salv〕*v.* 解決
on *one's* **own** 自行；獨自（= *by oneself*）
get lost 迷路　　*by oneself* 獨力；靠自己
sign〔saɪn〕*n.* 標誌；標示　　*figure out* 了解
plot〔plɑt〕*v.* 規劃　　route〔rut , raut〕*n.* 路線

Answer : Yes, but I wasn't very successful at solving it.

It involved two of my friends.

They had had a serious argument.

I tried to smooth things over.

I tried to get them to make up.

But I failed, and then they were both angry with me!

involve〔ɪn'vɑlv〕*v.* 包含；牽涉；和…有關
serious〔'sɪrɪəs〕*adj.* 嚴重的
argument〔'ɑrgjəmənt〕*n.* 爭論
smooth〔smuð〕*v.* 紓解；緩和 < *over* >
make up 和好

Question 9 ： *When it comes to giving gifts, people always say it is the thought that counts. Describe one special gift that you gave to someone.*

Answer ： I always find it hard to think of a gift for my mother.
I can't afford to buy the things she likes.
So Mother's Day I decided to give her time.

I gave her a gift certificate.
It was worth ten hours.
I promised to do ten hours of chores for her.

when it comes to + N/V-ing 一提到～　　count〔kaʊnt〕*v.* 重要
it is the thought that counts 心意最重要
find〔faɪnd〕*v.* 覺得　　hard〔hɑrd〕*adj.* 困難的
afford〔əˈfɔrd〕*v.* 負擔得起　　certificate〔səˈtɪfəkɪt〕*n.* 證書
gift certificate 禮券　　worth〔wɝθ〕*adj.* 有⋯價值的
chores〔tʃorz〕*n. pl.* 雜事；家事

Answer ： One of my friends collects model trains.
He's really into this hobby.
I knew that he had been looking for a particular train
　　for a while.

One day, when I was with my family in another town,
　　I saw it.
I immediately bought it, and then I kept it until his birthday.
He was thrilled when I gave it to him.

model〔ˈmɑdl̩〕*adj.* 模型的　　into〔ˈɪntʊ〕*prep.* 熱中⋯的
hobby〔ˈhɑbɪ〕*n.* 嗜好　　particular〔pɚˈtɪkjəlɚ〕*adj.* 特定的
for a while 一陣子　　thrilled〔θrɪld〕*adj.* 興奮的

Question 10 ： *Do you get on the Internet every day?　What do you do?*

Answer ： No, I don't use the Internet every day.

I don't have my own computer so it isn't that convenient.

I use the family computer in the living room.

My parents don't allow me to play games on it.

So I usually use the Internet to do homework.

I also send emails to my friends.

get on the Internet 上網 (= *use the Internet*)
allow 〔 ə'laʊ 〕 *v.* 允許
email 〔 'i,mel 〕 *n.* 電子郵件 (= *e-mail*)

Answer ： Yes, I get on the Internet every day.

It's part of my routine.

Checking my email is the first thing I do in the morning.

I also use the Net to do research.

It makes doing my homework much easier.

Last, I use it to chat with my friends.

It's part of… 是…的一部份 (= *It's a part of…*)
routine 〔 ru'tin 〕 *n.* 例行公事
the Net 網際網路 (= *the Internet*)
research 〔 'risɜtʃ , rɪ'sɜtʃ 〕 *n.* 研究
last 〔 læst 〕 *adv.* 【作為總結】最後　　chat 〔 tʃæt 〕 *v.* 聊天

第三部份：看圖敘述

1. This is a busy pedestrian street. It is in a Chinese country.

2. The people in the picture are walking along the street, shopping and looking at everything around them.

3. Yes. This looks a lot like one of our night markets, which I enjoy visiting very much.

4. The street is very crowded with people. There are lots of neon signs above their heads and on both sides of the road. On the right a vendor is selling food. In the center, a man and woman are holding hands as they walk. It looks like everyone is having a good time.

【註】busy〔'bɪzɪ〕*adj.* 熱鬧的　　pedestrian〔pə'dɛstrɪən〕*n.* 行人
night market 夜市　　***be crowded with*** 擠滿了
neon〔'niɑn〕*n.* 氖【一種稀有氣體，符號為 Ne】；霓虹燈
sign〔saɪn〕*n.* 招牌　　vendor〔'vɛndɚ〕*n.* 小販
hold hands 牽手　　***have a good time*** 玩得愉快

全民英語能力分級檢定測驗

中級英語檢定複試測驗⑩

寫作能力測驗

本測驗共有兩部份。第一部份為中譯英,第二部份為英文作文。測驗時間為**40分鐘**。

一、中譯英(**40%**)

說明:請將下列的一段中文翻譯成通順、達意且前後連貫的英文。

> 我最喜歡的活動之一是放風箏。放學後,只要天氣好,我就會跑到公園裡去放風箏。有一次我想試試看自己的風箏到底能飛多高。我綁了一捲又一捲的線,風箏果然飛得越來越高。風箏高到我都快看不見了。收回風箏之後,我花了一整個晚上在捲那些線。

二、英文作文(**60%**)

說明:請依下面所提供的文字提示寫一篇英文作文,長度約120字(8至12個句子)。作文可以是一個完整的段落,也可以分段。(評分重點包括內容、組織、文法、用字遣詞、標點符號、大小寫。)

提示:有些人害怕犯錯,但錯誤其實是我們最好的老師,因為我們常常是在錯誤中學習(Learning from a Mistake)。請寫一篇文章說明:

(1) 為何錯誤是有益的?

(2) 舉出你自己的經驗為例。

中級英檢寫作練習

口說能力測驗

請在 15 秒內完成並唸出下列自我介紹的句子：

My seat number is （複試座位號碼後 5 碼）, and my registration number is （初試准考證號碼後 5 碼）.

第一段份：朗讀短文

請先利用一分鐘的時間閱讀下面的短文，然後在二分鐘內以正常的速度，清楚正確的讀出下面的短文，閱讀時請不要發出聲音。

Cherry blossoms and camellias have begun to blossom in the mountains north of Taipei recently, a clear indication that Yangmingshan's flower season, and its many related activities, is on the way. The general public is invited to visit Yangmingshan to see the flowers. The camellia show will consist of an exhibition of various camellia strains and a display of pressed-flower art paintings created with dry materials taken from camellia plants.

*　　　　　　　*　　　　　　　*

Children learn almost nothing from television, and the more they watch the less they remember. They regard television purely as entertainment, dislike programs that demand their attention and are bewildered that anybody should take the medium seriously. Far from being overexcited by programs, they are mildly bored with the whole thing. These are the main conclusions from a new study of children and television. The author also confirms that the modern child is a devoted viewer. The study suggests that there is little point in the later hours. However, more than a third of the children regularly watch their favorite programs after 9 p.m. All eleven-year-olds have watched programs after midnight.

第二部份：回答問題

共十題。題目已事先錄音，每題經由耳機播出二次，不印在試卷上。第一至五題，每題回答時間 15 秒；第六至十題，每題回答時間 30 秒。每題播出後，請立即回答。回答時，不一定要用完整的句子，但請在作答時間內儘量的表達。

第三部份：看圖敘述

下面有一張圖片及四個相關的問題，請在一分半鐘內完成作答。作答時，請直接回答，不需將題號及題目唸出。

首先請利用 30 秒的時間看圖及問題。

1. 這可能是什麼地方？
2. 圖片中的人在做什麼？你認為這是什麼場合？
3. 你參加過這樣的活動嗎？你喜歡嗎？
4. 請敘述圖片中人物的穿著以及景物。

請將下列自我介紹的句子再唸一遍：

My seat number is（複試座位號碼後 5 碼）, and my registration number is（初試准考證號碼後 5 碼）.

口説能力測驗解答

第一部份：朗讀短文

請先利用一分鐘的時間閱讀下面二篇短文，閱讀時請不要發出聲音，然後在二分鐘之內以正常的速度，清楚正確的讀出下面的短文。

Cherry blossoms and camellias have begun to blossom in the mountains north of Taipei recently, a clear indication that Yangmingshan's flower season, and its many related activities, is on the way. The general public is invited to visit Yangmingshan to see the flowers. The camellia show will consist of an exhibition of various camellia strains and a display of pressed-flower art paintings created with dry materials taken from camellia plants.

【註】 cherry〔'tʃɛrɪ〕 n. 櫻桃；櫻桃樹
blossom〔'blɑsəm〕 n. 花　v. 開花
cherry blossom 櫻花
camellia〔kə'mɪlɪə〕 n. 山茶花
indication〔,ɪndə'keʃən〕 n. 顯示；跡象
season〔'sizṇ〕 n. 時期；季節　***flower season*** 花季
related〔rɪ'letɪd〕 adj. 相關的　***on the way*** 在途中；接近中
the (general) public 大衆；民衆　show〔ʃo〕 n. 展示會
consist of 由~組成；包含　exhibition〔,ɛksə'bɪʃən〕 n. 展覽
various〔'vɛrɪəs〕 adj. 各種的；各式各樣的
strain〔stren〕 n. 品種　display〔dɪ'sple〕 n. 展示
press〔prɛs〕 v. 壓　painting〔'pentɪŋ〕 n. 畫作
create〔krɪ'et〕 v. 創造　material〔mə'tɪrɪəl〕 n. 材料

Children learn almost nothing from television, and the more they watch the less they remember. They regard television purely as entertainment, dislike programs that demand their attention and are bewildered that anybody should take the medium seriously. Far from being overexcited by programs, they are mildly bored with the whole thing. These are the main conclusions from a new study of children and television. The author also confirms that the modern child is a devoted viewer. The study suggests that there is little point in the later hours. However, more than a third of the children regularly watch their favorite programs after 9 p.m. All eleven-year-olds have watched programs after midnight.

【註】 「the + 比較級…the + 比較級」表「越…就越…」。
regard A as B 視 A 為 B　　purely〔'pjʊrlɪ〕*adv.* 純粹地；全然地
entertainment〔ˌɛntə'tenmənt〕*n.* 娛樂
demand〔dɪ'mænd〕*v.* 需要　　attention〔ə'tɛnʃən〕*n.* 注意；專注
bewildered〔bɪ'wɪldəd〕*adj.* 困惑的
take sth. seriously 認真看待某事　　medium〔'midɪəm〕*n.* 媒體
far from 絕非　　overexcited〔'ovəɪk'saɪtɪd〕*adj.* 過份興奮的
mildly〔'maɪldlɪ〕*adv.* 溫和地；稍微
conclusion〔kən'kluʒən〕*n.* 結論
confirm〔kən'fɜm〕*v.* 證實；確認　　devoted〔dɪ'votɪd〕*adj.* 忠實的
viewer〔'vjuə〕*n.* 觀眾　　study〔'stʌdɪ〕*n.* 研究
suggest〔səg'dʒɛst〕*v.* 顯示　　point〔pɔɪnt〕*n.* 意義；作用
later hours 稍晚的時間　　*a third of* 三分之一
regularly〔'rɛgjələlɪ〕*adv.* 定期地　　midnight〔'mɪdˌnaɪt〕*n.* 半夜

第二部份：回答問題

Question 1 ： *Have you ever helped beggars on the street? Why or why not?*

Answer ： Yes, I sometimes give money to beggars.
I feel sorry for them.
I'd like to help.

To be honest, it's not much money to me.
It's just spare change.
But it might help them to eat for one day.

beggar〔'bɛgɚ〕*n.* 乞丐　　*feel sorry for* 同情
to be honest 老實說　　spare〔spɛr〕*adj.* 多餘的
change〔tʃendʒ〕*n.* 零錢

Answer ： No, I never give money to beggars.
I think that just encourages more begging.
People need to learn to help themselves.

That doesn't mean that I don't pity them.
I'm willing to help, but in a different way.
I prefer to support education and work programs for
　the poor.

encourage〔ɪn'kɝɪdʒ〕*v.* 鼓勵　　pity〔'pɪtɪ〕*v.* 同情
willing〔'wɪlɪŋ〕*adj.* 願意的　　work〔wɝk〕*v.* 擬定
program〔'progræm〕*n.* 計畫；方案
the poor 窮人（= *poor people*）

Question 2 ： *What is your religion? Are you a Buddhist or Christian or something else?*

Answer : I'm a Christian, and so are my brothers and sisters.
However, our parents and grandparents are Buddhists.
I think it's because we were sent to a Christian
elementary school.

In that place, we learned a lot about the religion.
It just seemed natural to adopt it.
Our parents don't mind, and they support our decision.

religion〔rɪ'lɪdʒən〕*n.* 宗教   Buddhist〔'budɪst〕*n.* 佛教徒
Christian〔'krɪstʃən〕*n.* 基督教徒
adopt〔ə'dɑpt〕*v.* 採用；採納   mind〔maɪnd〕*v.* 介意

Question 3 : *When you eat out, do you use your own chopsticks or
do you use disposable ones?*

Answer : I use the chopsticks in the restaurant.
Sometimes they are average chopsticks that need washing.
But many times they are disposable ones.

I know using disposable chopsticks is not
environmentally friendly, but it's convenient.
Bringing my own chopsticks everywhere is just
too much trouble.
I'd have to remember to wash them every night, too.

eat out 外出吃飯   chopsticks〔'tʃɑpˏstɪks〕*n. pl.* 筷子
disposable〔dɪ'spozəbl̩〕*adj.* 用完即丟的
average〔'ævərɪdʒ〕*adj.* 一般的；普通的
need + V-ing 需要被～ (= *need to be p.p.*)
time〔taɪm〕*n.* 次數   *environmentally friendly* 環保的

Question 4：*Do you often eat at home?　Why or why not?*

Answer：Yes, I often eat at home.

I live near my school, so it's convenient for me to go
　home for dinner.

Besides, my mom is a great cook!

But more than the food, I enjoy the family time.

We all sit around the table and talk while we eat.

This way we can keep up with what is going on in
　one another's lives.

cook〔kʊk〕*n.* 廚師　　***be a great cook***　很會做菜
this way　這樣一來　　***keep up with***　跟上；熟悉；了解
go on　發生

Answer：No, I rarely eat at home.

I'm just too busy to go home for dinner.

After school I grab a quick bite with my classmates.

Then we all head off to a cram school.

I never get home until after 10:00.

The only time I really spend with my family is on
　the weekend.

rarely〔'rɛrlɪ〕*adv.* 很少　　grab〔græb〕*v.* 抓住
bite〔baɪt〕*n.* 咬一口；食物　　***grab a bite***　吃點東西
head off　出發　　***cram school***　補習班
never⋯until~　每次都直到~才⋯【*not⋯until*　直到~才⋯】

Question 5：*Do you have a habit of eating late snacks?*

Answer：Yes, I often eat snacks at night.

I like to munch on something while I'm studying or
　watching TV.
It makes studying more fun!

People say it's a bad habit.
I know it's probably not very healthy, but it's hard to resist.
Luckily, I get a lot of exercise and can burn off the
　extra calories.

snack〔snæk〕*n.* 點心　　munch〔mʌntʃ〕*v.* 出聲地咀嚼 <*on*>
fun〔fʌn〕*adj.* 有趣的　　healthy〔'hɛlθɪ〕*adj.* 健康的
resist〔rɪ'zɪst〕*v.* 抵抗；抗拒
luckily〔'lʌkɪlɪ〕*adv.* 幸運地；幸好
burn off 燒掉；消耗　　calorie〔'kælərɪ〕*n.* 卡路里

Question 6 ： ***One of your friends invites you to go window-shopping,
but you don't want to. What will you say to decline the
invitation?***

Answer ： Thanks for the invitation.
I'd like to spend some time with you, but I don't really
　feel like window-shopping.
I just don't enjoy looking at things I can't afford.

Besides, it's always so crowded on Sundays.
Why don't we do something else?
How about getting a bite to eat or going to a movie?

go window-shopping 去逛街瀏覽櫥窗
decline〔dɪ'klaɪn〕*v.* 拒絕　　spend〔spɛnd〕*v.* 度過（時間）
feel like* + *V-ing 想要～　　afford〔ə'ford〕*v.* 負擔得起
crowded〔'kraʊdɪd〕*adj.* 擁擠的　　***How about* ～?** ～如何？
get a bite 吃點東西

Question 7 : *If you were a parent, would you send your preschool kid to a bilingual kindergarten?*

Answer : Yes, I would send my child to a bilingual kindergarten.

I think it would be a wonderful opportunity.

Children of that age can pick up a new language pretty quickly.

Besides, it would really help my child's pronunciation.

That would make a difference in the future.

It would give him or her a real advantage.

preschool〔 pri'skul 〕 *adj.* 學齡前的

bilingual〔 baɪ'lɪŋgwəl 〕 *adj.* 雙語的

kindergarten〔'kɪndəˌgɑrtn̩ 〕 *n.* 幼稚園

pick up 學會   pretty〔'prɪtɪ 〕 *adv.* 相當地

pronunciation〔 prəˌnʌnsɪ'eʃən 〕 *n.* 發音

make a difference 有差別；有影響

advantage〔 əd'væntɪdʒ 〕 *n.* 優點；優勢

Answer : No, I'd never send my child to a bilingual kindergarten.

I think kindergarten kids are too young to study.

They should spend their time playing and learning to socialize.

Having to learn another language could put pressure on them.

Besides, they might get the two languages confused.

Most of all, I think there is plenty of time to study in the future.

socialize〔'soʃəˌlaɪz 〕 *v.* 社交；交際

pressure〔'prɛʃə 〕 *n.* 壓力   ***put pressure on*** 對～施加壓力

confused〔 kən'fjuzd 〕 *adj.* 混淆的

most of all 最重要的是（= *most important of all*）
plenty of 很多的

Question 8：*Do you consider yourself a people person? Why or why not?*

Answer：Yes, I'm a people person.

I usually get along well with others.

I enjoy talking to them, and I think they like me too.

I'm good at persuading people.

I think I'd be good at a job that requires people skills.

Maybe I'll go into sales or become a good manager.

people person 喜歡接近人群的人；善交際的人
get along with sb. 與某人和諧相處　　*be good at* 擅長
persuade〔pə'swed〕v. 說服　　require〔rɪ'kwaɪr〕v. 需要
people skills 人際關係技巧　　*go into* 進入；從事

Answer：No, I don't consider myself a people person.

I often find it hard to understand others.

I can't figure out why they do the things they do.

This sometimes causes me problems when I have to
　work with others.

I think I'm too independent.

Maybe I'll become a scientist or writer.

consider〔kən'sɪdə〕v. 認為　　find〔faɪnd〕v. 覺得
figure out 了解　　*cause sb.* ～ 給某人帶來～
work with 和～合作　　independent〔ˌɪndɪ'pɛndənt〕adj. 獨立的

Question 9 : *Do you have a bank account? Do have a habit of saving money?*

Answer : Yes, I've had a bank account since I was in junior
　　　　　high school.
　　　　My parents helped me to open it.
　　　　They wanted me to learn how to handle money.

　　　　At first I just put in the money I got as gifts.
　　　　I always made a big deposit after the Lunar New Year!
　　　　Now I try to save a little bit of my pocket money
　　　　　every month.

account〔ə'kaʊnt〕*n.* 帳戶　　save〔sev〕*v.* 存（錢）
open an account 開戶　　handle〔'hænd!〕*v.* 處理；應付
at first 起初　　***put in*** 存（錢）　　deposit〔dɪ'pɑzɪt〕*n.* 存款
Lunar New Year 農曆新年　　***pocket money*** 零用錢

Question 10 : *Do you have any experiences of being with a little baby?*

Answer : Yes, I've taken care of my older sister's baby a few times.
　　　　Now he is nearly two years old, but my sister often asked
　　　　　me to help her when he was an infant.
　　　　At first I was nervous, but then I got used to it.

　　　　Taking care of a little baby is a big responsibility.
　　　　They depend on adults for everything!
　　　　I think I've learned a lot from the experience.

take care of 照顧　　nearly〔'nɪrlɪ〕*adv.* 將近
infant〔'ɪnfənt〕*n.* 嬰兒　　nervous〔'nɝvəs〕*adj.* 緊張的
get used to + N/V-ing 習慣於～
responsibility〔rɪˌspɑnsə'bɪlətɪ〕*n.* 責任
depend on 依賴　　adult〔ə'dʌlt〕*n.* 成人

第三部份：看圖敘述

1. This is a swimming pool.

2. The boys are practicing swimming, and their teacher or coach is helping them. I think this is a swimming class.

3. Yes, I had to take swimming classes in high school. I did not like it very much because it was always cold.

4. Several boys are lined up to dive into the pool. Others are already in the water. The boys are wearing swimming caps and goggles. Their teacher is standing beside the pool adjusting one of the swimmers' goggles. In the background, there several white chairs and a boy is waiting there.

【註】 coach〔kotʃ〕*n.* 教練　　***line up*** 排隊
dive〔daɪv〕*v.* 跳水　　pool〔pul〕*n.* 游泳池（= *swimming pool*）
cap〔kæp〕*n.* 帽子；泳帽　　goggles〔'gɑglz〕*n. pl.* 護目鏡；蛙鏡
beside〔bɪ'saɪd〕*prep.* 在～旁邊　　adjust〔ə'dʒʌst〕*v.* 調整
background〔'bæk,graʊnd〕*n.* 背景